KILLERS' GAME

Bannister sent a blast of gunfire to cut Webb's words. He fell to the floor, rolling against the wall. Despairingly he remembered his promise to Martha that Bannister would not be killed. There was only one thing to do then and that was to pretend that Bannister's treachery had worked. Rolling over on his face, he groaned softly and lay still.

There was a long silence, and then Bannister came forward. Webb heard him halt above him, and now he felt Bannister's boot in his side, trying to toe him over. Webb relaxed, giving slackly against the pressure of the boot. It was dark here, and Webb knew that Bannister would strike a match to make sure he was dead. The only question was, would he shoot a second time before he struck the match?

MARAUDERS' MOON

LUKE SHORT

A DELL BOOK

Published by
DELL PUBLISHING CO., INC.
1 Dag Hammarskjold Plaza
New York, N.Y. 10017

ISBN: 0-440-15326-3

Previous Dell Editions #B130 and #5326
New Dell Edition
First printing—March 1978

I_F "I_{RON} H_{AT}" P_{ETTY} had not been so mad when he climbed the windmill tower behind the O. K. corral, he might have seen it. He didn't, though. He ignored the shadeless and wind-bitten main street of Wagon Mound below and, with a length of bailing wire in his free hand, turned to the splintered pump shaft and cursed.

So the men on each of the four main corners of town went unnoticed. Not that they weren't obvious to the people on the street—and there were many of them—but Iron Hat would have read some order into their placement. If he had seen them, he would have immediately noticed they wore the straight-brimmed, low-crowned, and dented Stetsons of the Montana country. And seeing this, he would have studied them closer, noting that the man catty-corner from the bank stood at the tie-rail in front of three big-boned and sleek north country horses. Across the side street from him and leaning against the front of the sheriff's office, the second man was slowly rolling a cigarette. The third, catty-corner from him, lounged on the tie-rail before two ground-haltered horses. The fourth man Iron Hat could not have seen, because he was leaning against the bank wall under the big window, looking up and down the street.

Seeing this man, Iron Hat could have guessed where the fifth man was, but he didn't see. About to climb down the ladder after a tool, Iron Hat only looked out on the broad plain surrounding the town. He saw two riders just entering on the east road, and he did notice that instead of riding abreast, they rode in single file. Iron Hat guessed right this time, because, even though he couldn't make out the rifle across the saddle of the man in the rear, he knew it was there, and he wondered idly and without much interest, as an old man will, what prisoner was being brought in.

The man holding the rifle across his thighs could have told Iron Hat it was Webb Cousins. He could have told him that he'd ridden close to a hundred and fifty miles, and across a wide desert, to get him, but very likely he would not have answered any one's questions now. He was a short-tempered deputy at this moment.

"Pull up, Cousins," he said to the man ahead.

The man on the big roan reined in and looked back over his shoulder, presenting to the deputy sheriff of Wintering County, the next to the south, a lean and sober face with a rash of freckles across the cheeks and forehead. He might have been twenty-six. His fists, resting folded on the saddle horn, were square, bony, like the set of his overbroad shoulders under the faded blue shirt, wet with perspiration. His dusty Stetson was pushed back a little, so that it rode at a careless angle atop a thick thatch of red hair; and his worn Levis and scuffed cowboots contrived, with the Stetson, to give him an air of a man not over troubled by what was waiting for him. Rain gray and mocking eyes under thick eyebrows followed the approach of the deputy, whose carbine was cocked, pointed.

"Put out your hand," the deputy said surlily, at the same time fumbling in his saddlebags for a pair of handcuffs, which he eventually brought out.

Cousins drawled, "You readin' palms now?"

There was something in the sleep-famished eyes and harried heavy face of the deputy that was just as ugly as his voice. With a quick gesture, he looped the cuffs over the saddle horn and palmed up a worn six-gun, which he cocked and leveled at Cousins, sheathing his carbine with the other hand.

"The poster said alive or dead. Take your choice," Deputy McWilliams said.

Cousins said nothing.

"I said, 'Put out your hand.'"

Cousins crossed his right hand over and held it out.

"The other, damn you!"

Webb complied, grinning faintly. McWilliams locked Webb's left wrist to his own right, thus placing his carbine and six-gun, both holstered on the left side, farthest from Cousins. McWilliams was a heavy man, middle-aged, inclined to weight, some of which was in his full fighter's jaw. He tipped back his battered Stetson now, and regarded Webb with angry distaste.

"I may not get away with this," he said slowly, sourly. "They don't like us over in this county. But I can make you one promise. If they get snaky with me, you're a dead man."

Webb frowned and jerked his head toward the town. "Ain't this where we're headed for?"

"No. We're one county too far north."

"And they don't like you here?"

"No. We've been known to shoot each other on sight." Webb stared at him. "Then why go in?"

McWilliams sighed and glared at him. "A man can stand only so much. I'm dead for sleep, and I got to have a jail for you. I'll take a chance. So will you."

"Sure."

"All right. Come along."

They traveled on down the dusty road of the county-seat town, which passed a few pole corrals and shacks before it dived immediately into the two blocks of wooden-awninged stores flanking the fetlock-deep dust of the street. In the saddle, side by side, Cousins was not the bigger of these two men, but he was the taller, and even that may have been because he sat his saddle flatly and erectly. Or again, it may have been because, for the last three nights, he had slept deep and restfully, while Mc-Williams stayed awake to guard him.

Approaching the four corners of Wagon Mound, Webb noticed a scattering of buckboards at the hitch-rack, and many saddle horses, but these appeared to be concentrated in front of the Lady Gay Saloon next to the bank.

He observed the four corners curiously, at once identifying the sheriff's office on one corner, and then his attention settled on the man standing before it. Something in this man's attitude, his clothes, made Webb look across the street to the man leaning against the bank. Curiosity building in him, Webb turned his head and looked into the face of the man not fifteen feet from him, who was lounging against the tie-rail in front of two ground-haltered horses. Their glances met for a second, and both were hard, curious, the man's quietly menacing, Webb's faintly amused. To complete the picture, Webb looked across at the other corner. There was the fourth man. And Webb Cousins smiled.

Pulling up in front of the sheriff's office, Deputy Mc-Williams started to swing his leg over the saddle to dismount when he felt the tug of the handcuffs at his right wrist. He settled back in the saddle again, confronted with the necessity of dismounting on the right side of his horse or unlocking the handcuffs.

"That's what I was trying to tell you back there," Webb said quietly.

The deputy glared at him.

Webb lowered his voice. "And you better do it quick, mister."

The deputy scowled. He sat there a moment longer, puzzled, then he swung his left leg up and almost fell out of the saddle on the right side of his horse. Trained to one way of mounting and dismounting, and that on his left side, the horse looked back, then started to pitch before McWilliams's feet were on the ground. The deputy stumbled away, and would have fallen had it not been for Webb yanking him up by the handcuffs. The man smoking before the sheriff's office smiled narrowly. He had a match in the corner of his mouth, and he spoke around it. "Pretty," he remarked.

McWilliams heard him, but he pretended not to. He said to Cousins, "Get down."

Webb dismounted. They swung under the tie-rail, wrist to wrist, just as the door of the sheriff's office opened and a thick-bodied, burly man stepped out onto the single step. He slowly put his hands on his hips and spread his legs. His black saber mustaches seemed to bristle, and his eyes narrowed.

"Well, well, a Winterin' County deputy," he drawled in an ugly tone to McWilliams. "This is what you'd call a—"

He never finished. From the depths of the bank a sharp, echoing report blasted out. The man with the match in his mouth, the man Webb had been watching, straightened up and lounged erect, and when both his feet were on the boardwalk, there was a gun in his hand.

He pointed it toward the burly man in the door. "Get back in the clock, birdie," he said flatly to the burly man.

From across the street in the bank door there was a hurried tattoo of footsteps, those of a man running. The man with the gun did not look over; he was looking at the burly man and there was an unpleasant smile behind the match.

Deputy McWilliams glanced hurriedly over his shoulder, saw the man with the heavy gunny sack streaking across the road, and then he said heavily, surprised, "Hey, that man stuck up—"

"Sure," the gunman said quietly, jeeringly. "Why don't you try and bulldog him?" But he never looked at McWilliams. He was walking toward the man in the door, who was stepping gingerly back into the office.

McWilliams took one swift look at the gunman, saw his back half turned, and went for his gun.

The holdup guard across the street was watching this. When he saw McWilliams's hand drop, he raised his own Colt, leveled it, took careful sight, and shot. McWilliams's back arched and he fell forward, his weight dragging Webb with him. Webb, pulled to his knees, saw the hole in McWilliams's back and he looked up at the jeering gunman not six feet from him.

"You want out of them things, son?" the gunman asked.

"No. Thanks."

"Okay. I only asked," the gunman said. He swiveled his gun now and sent one swift shot through the batwing doors of the Lady Gay across the street, then he grinned at Webb, who now was sitting on the lone step of the sheriff's office. The guard against the bank threw a shot over Webb's head into the door of the office, then ran.

The gunman beside Webb looked swiftly upstreet, saw that three of his confederates were mounted and waiting there. He reached up with his gun, broke the window of the sheriff's office above him and shot once at its ceiling.

"So long, bud," he said to Webb, and ran for his horse.

In another eight seconds, the five of them were galloping out of town. Only then did the men in the Lady Gay begin to boil out of its doors. There were shouts, a frantic milling of horses.

CHAPTER TWO

BEHIND WEBB, the burly man bellowed unnecessarily, "They went south! Every man get a horse!".

Out of the moil of horses and dust and running men, three horsemen broke away, and were at a gallop as they passed the bank. Then some order seemed to come out of the milling and the whole street was filled with men riding south. Even the merchants joined the posse; one man in a white apron, hatless, cursing, brought his horse out of a rear and joined the race.

In another minute the thunder had passed, leaving a fog of dust in the canyon of the main street, and a silence that settled even more quickly.

Webb saw a derbied, shambling man, Iron Hat Petty, leave the archway of the O. K. corral and pause to talk with the aproned bartender of the Lady Gay. As they looked up the street, the swing doors were shouldered open, and a gaunt, hunched man, who handled his single crutch like a second leg, swung out past them and started toward the bank. Halfway there, he saw Webb sitting on the doorstep of the sheriff's office, and he hesitated, then swung under the hitch-rack and crossed the street.

Closer to him now, Webb saw the star of the sheriff's office on his vest, which was as careless and worn as his Stetson and Levis. His right leg was shorter than his left, and the foot was twisted out, encased in a boot with an unworn sole.

He stopped in front of Webb, and the kindly look in his pale eyes was clouded with wonder as he silently observed McWilliams on his face, the locked handcuffs, and then Webb.

"I know that man, don't I?" he asked Webb.

"McWilliams, over in the next county."

The sheriff nodded. His spare face, with its weathered skin so close to the skull, changed just a little with wonder.

"Dead, is he?"

"Yes."

The sheriff nodded. "Well, that's one good thing come out of this. Turn him over."

Webb did, and the sheriff took one swift look at him. Then he settled his attention on Webb.

"What was he doin' here?"

"He wanted to borrow your jail for me. Needed sleep, I reckon."

The sheriff shifted his crutch a little. "Well, take them things off. You can't drag him around." He paused. "What'd he want of you?"

Webb grinned. "He had a great big sack he wanted me to hold."

"For what?"

"About two years back there was a train robbery over south of Bull Foot in Wintering County."

"I remember it."

"I was ridin' the train. When the law couldn't find the outfit that did it, they claimed it was an inside job. Said so on the reward posters." Webb gestured over east. "I was workin' across the desert over yonder. One day this McWilliams shows up with a bench warrant. So I'm here."

"But this ain't Wintering County," the sheriff said gently, "so take 'em off."

When Webb was free of the handcuffs, the sheriff signaled him to follow and headed across the street for the bank.

As they were mounting the steps, the sheriff noted the man standing in the door and he grunted. The man gestured inside with his thumb and said in a quiet snarl, which barely changed the hard angle of his face:

"There it is, Wardecker. Patton's dead, and the bank's cleaned—to the last dollar."

He had a natural truculence of speech and manner that goes with a small man, but it went beyond that. Small, hardbitten, with a tight, tough, grizzled face, the man spoke as if he had been waiting for this moment to blame the sheriff for this and a hundred other things that rankled him. He was dressed in the clothes of cattleland, but with a difference, Webb saw. The gun on his hip was pearl-handled with gold inlay; his boots were tooled leather, handsewn; his trousers of a cloth that was rich and expensive, if soiled. The only untidy thing about him was his greasy Stetson, battered and almost ragged, and his shirt, blue and worn and patched. His stance, erect, belligerent, was without the gentleness that his graying hair would indicate.

He made a small, impotent gesture of wrath as he finished speaking.

"Sure," Sheriff Wardecker said. "They knew their business."

"Do something, man!" the smaller man exploded.

The sheriff turned a speculative gaze on him. "There's a posse not three minutes behind 'em, Buck. You got a horse, haven't you?"

"Which way'd they go?"

"South," the sheriff said quietly, wryly. "They're headin' for Wintering County, you can bet. And once they cross the line, they'll be safe."

The small man said in quiet fury, "Wintering County! Sure! Safe as a church! All they got to do is walk right in under the nose of our law and clean us out, then jump over into Wintering." He glared up at the sheriff, his jaw outthrust, his face flushed with anger.

"This feud wasn't of my makin', Buck," the sheriff said. He turned and walked into the bank, Webb following him. The story of the robbery was there for anyone to read. Behind the high counter just outside the wire cashier's cage, a middle-aged, heavy man lay sprawled on the floor in a pool of blood. Standing against the wall was a pale young man, watching them. Beside the desk was a coil of rope. Inside the wire cage, against the back wall, the safe door was open, and on the floor around it was a scattering of papers.

The little man said from beside Webb, "I was talkin' to Patton when this holdup fella walked in and poked a gun in my back, and told Patton what he wanted. I went for my gun, when he slugged me from behind. Patton went for his, too. This hardcase shot him. He had a coil of rope with him, aimin' to tie Poole here up, but after the shot, he jumped the counter and slugged Poole, too. But he took his time with the safe. Cleaned it out."

The sheriff nodded and said to the clerk, "You better go get a drink of whisky, son, then get some help and take Patton home."

It was a gesture of finality that seemed to turn the small man's anger into a sort of bleak despair. He turned away from the sight and said to Wardecker, "Well, this'll mean the ruin of a good part of the county."

"How much was took?"

"Poole says in the neighborhood of seventy-five thousand."

"Uh-huh," Wardecker said softly. "Fifty families of us cleaned out because we got a county next to us that won't lift a hand to help us and will likely be glad because it happened." He regarded the smaller man quizzically. "This here row comes to about what I claimed it would, don't it, Buck?"

Buck Tolleston recaptured some of his anger.

"I've listened to that preachin' for ten years, War-decker! But damned if I'll listen to it now!"

"Sure," Wardecker said mildly. For a moment Tolles-ton glared at him, and then his gaze swiveled to Webb. "Who the hell are you?" he demanded savagely.

"Wait a minute," the sheriff said. He told Tolleston about Webb, and about the shooting of McWilliams.

"And you never saw this comin'?" Tolleston asked Webb slowly. "You was out there on the street, and rode right past those hardcases and didn't see it?"

"I saw it," Webb said coldly. "Hell, anyone with eyes could have."

"And you never done nothin'?"

"Like what?"

"Holler, shoot, anything to bust it up!" Tolleston said hotly.

"I was handcuffed to this lawman," Webb said slowly. "If I'd opened my mouth, I'd of got it four ways."

Tolleston's mouth sagged in amazement, and Webb could almost read what was passing through his mind. For Tolleston, had he been in Webb's place, would have shouted a warning and been killed for his pains, and it would have been instinctive, unheeding of danger, an act of a terrier who is bred to fight and die. The little man turned to the sheriff. "You heard that, Will?"

"I heard it."

Tolleston said, "What kind of—" He paused, breathing hard, and said more quietly, "Maybe I don't understand this."

To Webb he said, "So they wanted you for robbin' a train? Are you sure we don't want you along with them other five hardcases that got away with the money?"

Webb flushed. "Sure. You want all of us. McWilliams was in on it. He just rode past four of us and let us hold up your bank because he don't like this county. As soon as I get loose, I'll join the boys and we'll blow your seventy-five thousand on kewpie dolls."

Tolleston exploded. His left arm drove straight into Webb's face, slamming him into the counter. Slowly Webb raised a hand to his mouth and he did not look at the sheriff as he said thickly, "Is it all right if I go ahead?"

"It's Buck's fight," Wardecker said.

Tolleston came at Webb again. This time Webb was ready, and there was no gentleness in what he did. With open hand he whipped through Tolleston's flailing fists, and the smack of his palm on the smaller man's face was like a gunshot. Driving into him, he grabbed both of Tolleston's upper arms and pinned them to his side, and the veins in Webb's temples swelled with effort to quell his writhing. Then sharply, heaving, he lifted Tolleston to the counter, sat him there, and fisted his raised hand.

"You're near an old man," Webb said thickly. "But if you ask for any more, you'll get it."

His face livid with rage, Tolleston struck out again. Webb dodged it and at the same time hooked viciously at Tolleston's face. The smaller man pinwheeled over the counter, landed with a thud on his side, skidded, and was brought up sharply against the far wall.

Very slowly, shaking his head, he dragged himself erect.

Wardecker said, "Don't go for a gun, Buck. I'm warnin' you."

Tolleston looked dazedly at them both, and suddenly his weathered face broke into a wry smile.

"I reckon I had that comin'," he murmured. "But it don't change things a bit."

Webb hitched up his pants and his bony face was hard with anger, and with a vast and ungovernable impatience.

"I've had about enough of this rawhiding," he said

flatly, sharply. "I let that tinhorn deputy drag me across the desert because I knew I was innocent and I was tired of where I was. I figured it was an easy frame-up to dodge. But I don't aim to get hoorawed like the runt in the litter. And if you boys here think you can kick me around, somebody's going to get bit." He looked at the sheriff. "Either of you," he added.

The sheriff's eyes glinted a little, and possibly with amusement. Three men and the clerk stepped through the door of the bank just then and found Webb glaring belligerently at the other two.

"Better come over to the office," Wardecker said mildly. "Both of you."

CHAPTER THREE

As THEY REACHED THE SIDEWALK, Webb saw the ʾurly man with the black mustaches hand the reins of his horse over to Iron Hat Petty, who led him down the street to the corral. The man went inside the sheriff's office and in a few moments they joined him.

The room was small, containing besides a few rickety chairs, an oversize desk with a top crisscrossed by spur scars. The walls were plastered with yellowed and fly-specked reward posters. Wardecker motioned Tolleston and Webb to seats, then addressed the other man.

"What happened, Wally?"

"I dunno," the deputy answered glumly. "My pony threw a shoe, and I had to pull out of it." He swore feelingly. "Hell, they'll never catch that outfit before they cross into Wintering. Did you see the horses they was ridin'?"

Wardecker sighed and said he didn't. Wally described them—big, rangy, almost two hands higher than the native stock—and while he talked, Webb observed him. The importance of his office sat heavily on him, Webb guessed, for he was sober, almost pompous, his heavy mustaches adding to this impression. He was everything a deputy should be, Webb thought; a man to take orders but never think of them, a man, thorough and slow and dull.

Tolleston was listening to Wally's conversation and finally, when his impatience mastered him, cut in with:

"All right, all right. They had big horses. They're in Wintering already. Now, sheriff, let's get down to business." He glared at Webb. "I want to know all about this."

Patiently Wardecker reiterated his discovery of Webb sitting on the doorstep chained to the dead McWilliams's wrist.

"That's right," Wally put in. "I was talking to Mc-Williams when I heard the shot."

"What'd you do then?" the sheriff asked.

"The hardcase leaning against the wall told me to get back to the office. Then I heard another shot. That must have been the one that got McWilliams."

Tolleston exploded. "What's it got to do with the facts? I say McWilliams and this man were part of the outfit that was in town waiting to stick up the bank. McWilliams brought this man in hoping that he'd tie up the whole bunch of you in a row while the bank was robbed!"

Webb did not seem to be the only one surprised by this news. Sheriff Wardecker raised up in his seat and said, "Buck, quit that."

Wally looked again at Webb, and over his rather stupid face came an expression of surprise, mingled with thoughtfulness. He studied Webb carefully a moment, then he said to Tolleston, "If that's true, Buck, why did these men shoot McWilliams?"

"Why, you blasted fool—so they only had to split the loot six ways instead of seven. Besides, being a peace officer, he could turn right around and betray them for the reward, once this county posted it!" He looked at Webb, his eyes hot with anger.

Webb slowly rose out of his chair, and Wally stepped up to him.

"Sit down, fella," he said curtly.

Webb brushed him aside, and stood stiffly in front of

Tolleston. "Why, you little, dried-up, big-eared counter jumper, have I got to slap that mouth o' yours shut or will you let the sheriff talk?"

Webb felt his arms pinned behind him y Wally. He struggled wrathfully to get away, but W. ly held him tightly. Wardecker, who had been observi g this with sleepy, thoughtful immobility, drew out l s pipe and knocked it out and said, "Sit down, Red. You ren't hung yet."

Webb subsided and sat down in his chair, ut Tolleston's tight, fighting face had not changed a jo. He said calmly to Webb, "That was a frame-up, backed by Wintering County. They even sent their deputy to help pull it off."

Wally suddenly snapped his fingers and turned an accusing face to Webb.

"Didn't I hear you talkin' to that gunman that covered me?"

"Sure. He asked me if I wanted those cuffs off."

"Why?" Tolleston rapped out.

Webb's annoyance was almost anger. "Dammit, men like that are against all law! He wanted to free me! Anything wrong with that?"

Tolleston looked over at the sheriff. "Is there, Wardecker?" he asked mockingly.

"Not that I can see," Wardecker said calmly. "This man didn't take the offer."

"He didn't have time."

Webb said in savage exasperation, "I'm the only man that saw this! McWilliams, like a damn fool, went for his gun, and one of those hardcases across the street cut down on him. He fell. This hardcase asked me if I wanted loose. I didn't want any part of it, and I told him so. I sat still and minded my own business, when I could have got loose and run with those hombres." He looked around the room. "What's this all about? Have you got to saddle this thing on the first stranger that rides into town?"

Tolleston waited until he was finished, then, ignoring everything Webb had said, he addressed the sheriff.

"Wardecker, I've lived too long in this place not to know that outfit next door. Wintering County planned this, and Wintering County pulled it off. Why, a blind man could see it. There ain't been a Wintering County deputy in Wagon Mound for ten years. He'd of been shot if he showed his face here. All right, our bank was stuck up. This deputy not only comes in on the day the bank was held up, but he come in the very hour and minute of the stick-up! He knew he could tie up every lawman in town in a row with him while the bank was held up. I almost broke up the plan, so they had to hurry." He jabbed a blunt finger in Webb's direction. "This man is guilty of sharing in this bank robbery. And if you don't aim to hold him for trial, I'll swear out a warrant for him myself!"

"On what grounds?" Wardecker drawled.

"I just told you! For aidin' this bank robbery. I own the biggest block of stock in the bank, and I've got to protect the depositors."

The sheriff stared absently at his pipe and then laid it on the desk top. He looked up and said gently to Tolleston, "I won't do it, Buck."

"You got to!"

"I don't reckon. There's got to be grounds before you can swear out a warrant. There ain't sufficient grounds in this case."

Tolleston glared wrathfully at the sheriff, his face so deep a red that Webb was waiting for him to explode. Surprisingly, he began to talk, and mildly, too. "Wardecker, you admit you got a right to hold a man on suspicion. You done it time and again, when you ain't sure of a man."

"Sure."

"All right. Will you hold this man till I get proof of my suspicions?"

Wardecker scratched his chin and thought a moment. "All right."

Webb half rose out of his seat to protest when Wally shoved him back. Tolleston turned to Webb.

"You ain't got enough money to meet bail, have you?"

"You know I haven't!" Webb said hotly.

Buck turned to the sheriff. "All right. Throw him in, Wardecker."

"Not so fast," Wardecker said slowly to Buck. "All the county funds was in the bank, Buck, and they're stolen. It'll cost a dollar a day to feed this man if I throw him in jail. I don't aim to run the county in debt, so I don't aim to throw him in jail." He leaned back and picked up his pipe and drawled, "You force me to run that 'arrest on suspicion' sandy, Buck, and I'll hide behind my rights. Take your choice."

"But that ain't arrestin' him if you don't lock him up!" Tolleston said hotly.

"That's pretty plain."

Tolleston was mute with wrathful impotence. He sat down and stared at Wardecker, his mouth open to protest. Suddenly he closed it and yanked a sack of tobacco from his pocket and rolled a smoke. Halfway through it, he looked up and said, "And you won't guard him, either, I reckon?"

Wardecker said, "There's no county law makin' me walk around with a prisoner handcuffed to my wrist, is there?"

Buck dropped his cigarette. "Wardecker, I'm one of the county commissioners. I'm goin' to call them together and make 'em force you to put this man in jail!"

"It'll take three days," the sheriff said imperturbably.

"All right. And since we can't let the man escape, I reckon it falls on me to make sure of it."

"I wondered when you'd see that."

"All right. I'll take him with me. I'll take him out to the ranch—"

"And you won't lock him up and you'll feed him good, and you'll exercise a reasonable judgment in havin' him watched," Wardecker interrupted mildly. "If you don't promise it, you don't take the prisoner."

"Reasonable?" Buck echoed. "Like what?"

"Like putting him to work and feedin' him proper and not lockin' him up. Of course, you can't let him carry a gun. I wouldn't let him near a good horse. But that'll be easy."

"And if I won't do it?"

"Then you'll have to leave him in town," Wardecker told him. He looked over at Webb, a glint of amusement in his eye. "How does that sound to you, son?"

"Like a frame-up," Webb said curtly.

"No, it ain't," Wardecker said. "What I'm tryin' to turn it into is a job. It'll take Buck from now till judgment day to prove what he suspects. I don't even know how he's goin' to go about it. But I do know I ain't holdin' an innocent man in jail till he does. You'll go with him. He can't lock you up, and he can't starve you. But he can give you work and food and shelter, what you'd get out of any job. And when Buck finds he can't get the proof he wants, he's goin' to pay you for your work, just like any other man. Ain't that so, Buck?"

"I won't have to pay him," Buck said shortly.

"We'll see."

Tolleston regarded Webb with grim-jawed suspicion. "If I can't lock him up, Buck, what's to prevent him from stealin' a horse and high-tailin' it?"

"Because I'm goin' to keep his own horse," Wardecker said. "That means you'll have to mount him, Buck. If he jumps the country, I'll notify every sheriff's office in the Territory."

He pointed a blunt finger at Tolleston. "And if you don't know this by now, Buck, you ought to. If a man's got a reward on his head for a crime—bank robbery, say, or murder—a lawman will break his neck to get him alive and collect the reward. But in this Territory, if a man's wanted for horse stealing, he's headed for a hang-noose. And I'll tell you why. Because the reward's small, and because a lawman'll figure that if a man was wanted for murder, he might've had a reason for doin' it. But if he steals horses, prison ain't goin' to cure him. A rope—or a shot in the back will."

Tolleston nodded.

"So I don't think you'll steal a horse," Wardecker said to Webb. To Buck he said, "All right, there's your new hand, Buck."

CHAPTER FOUR

Tolleston left orders for Webb to stay there till he returned, then stomped out, Wally following him, to get help in disposing of McWilliams's body. Once they were gone, Webb walked over and confronted Wardecker. He cuffed back his Stetson so that his shock of red hair darkly framed his creased forehead and his scowl, and put his hands on his hips.

"I want to get this straight," he drawled. "Are you the sheriff around here, or do you just wear that star because you got a hole in your vest?"

Wardecker picked up his pipe and packed it this time and answered presently "Yes, I'm the sheriff. Why?"

"And you don't think I was mixed up in this stick-up. Leastways, you been on my side so far."

"Yes."

"But you don't believe it enough that you'll go the whole hog and free me. You'd like to keep me around here for those boys to work their steam off on, and as soon as they cool down, I can ride on my way, huh? Easier on you. Somebody's got to be the sucker, huh?"

"Easy, son," Wardecker said gently. "I—"

"Easy, hell! What kind of county is this that'll take another county's prisoner and carpenter a nice shiny new frame-up on him when he's just passing through?" Webb said hotly. "I could understand it if it was going to do Wintering County any harm! You'd blame Wintering

County if the moon didn't rise when you want it to, but I'm damned if I see how this is goin' to hurt them! And if it ain't that you're usin' me for a snubbin' post, and if it ain't that you're hurtin' Wintering County, just why am I being held?"

"You heard Tolleston, didn't you?"

Webb scoffed. "That half-pint fake! He don't believe hisself."

Wardecker took the pipe from his mouth and shook his head. "You're wrong there, son. He believes you're in it. He sta....d this bank, and it was mostly with his own money. Folks believed in him, so they put their with his."

"But—"

"And he thinks you were in on it. Buck Tolleston ain' always fair, but he's as fair as a bull-headed, hot-tempered man can be," Wardecker cut in. Then he smiled. "You'l like him, I reckon. And he'll like you."

"We like each other already," Webb said dryly. "Didn't you see him offer me a job? Just like they offer bad men a job down South—workin' on a road. Only they chain 'em there, and the prison gets their wages."

"You'd rather go to jail?"

Webb checked himself. "Well, no," he said slowly. "But if I got to be railroaded—and I reckon I do—I'd a sight rather it wouldn't be by a big wind like him."

"Why?"

"Why? If he ever gets me outside this town, he'll probably shoot me. I just don't like bein' shot that's all!"

Wardecker sighed patiently. "He's made mistakes, but he won't make that one."

Webb snorted in disgust and fell back into a chair. "So he has made mistakes? I'm surprised to hear it—a great big, all-knowin', certain-sure eyeful of a man like him."

Wardecker saw the worst was over, but he went right on: "That's just the trouble. He made a mistake ten years ago he'll be payin' for for some time to come."

"I'm glad to hear that," Webb said sourly, but his anger was fading.

"Maybe you won't be. I got a hunch you're goin' to get tolled in on that mistake, just like the rest of us."

Webb looked up curiously from the cigarette he was building. What did the old man mean by that?

Wardecker saw that flicker of interest. "I mean this row between Wintering County and us, San Patricio. You'll get dragged into it. Every man that lives here is in it."

"I'm in it now," Webb said. "I reckon you and Wintering will be fightin' from now on to see who has the chance to frame me."

"That won't happen. Buck Tolleston is just using you as an excuse to blame Wintering County, like he'd blame a bad blizzard on them if he could."

"What's the matter with him," Webb asked disgustedly. "Is he crazy?"

"On one subject."

"But why?"

"You'd have to understand the basin here to know that. Know anything about this country?"

"I don't even want to."

But Wardecker went on talking, as if he hadn't heard. "Well, over on the west and north is the Frying Pans, and beyond that the desert. Over on the east—stretchin' for fifty-odd miles south—is the Silver Horn Breaks. This here basin proper, includin' both San Patricio County and Wintering County, is about sixty miles by ninety. But Wintering County is to the south. It has the railroad, and better range than San Patricio." He paused. "Buck Tolleston used to own that—nearly half of Wintering County—a cattle kingdom."

Webb showed a faint interest now, but he would not betray it out of stubbornness.

Wardecker, sensing this, continued: "Buck was chased out of Texas twenty years ago by the Bannister outfit. He drove a herd of longhorns up here and settled, but the Bannisters followed him."

"I'm glad of that," Webb growled. "I wish they'd chased him farther."

Wardecker went on to explain the growth of the feud between the two counties. Bannister and his relations packed the Wintering County offices with themselves and their men and then passed the cattle-inspection law which was the downfall of Buck Toleston.

"I don't see that," Webb said slowly. "Every county has got an inspection law."

"Sure. But not like this one. The trail herds was just beginning to go north, then, and Buck was the first to send his herds up. Then Wake Bannister and his men rammed through this inspection law. But instead of chargin' the usual rate of inspection for all cattle leavin' the county—ten cents a head for the first hundred and three for all over—they charged five dollars a head for the first hundred and three dollars for all over. Of course, it was revenge on Buck Tolleston, and it wasn't enforced against any other man. But it drove Buck out."

"To here?"

"Yes. Him and his friends. I was one of 'em. We blocked out this county in the upper basin and figured to drive stuff out any way but south." He smiled wryly. "And then's when we cut our own throats."

Webb asked why.

"North and west you got a desert just over the mountains. East you got the Silver Horn Breaks, with no water. By the time your herd is half through it their feet are bleedin'. You're lucky if you get a fifth of your herd through alive. And we can't go south through Wintering."

"But the railroad," Webb said. "Ain't there a railroad

in Wintering that runs to Bull Foot?"

"No San Patricio man could reach it with a dozen head. They'd kill him. That's Wake Bannister's way of punishing Buck Tolleston and us. So we sit here bush-whackin' over the county line, refusing to return each other's prisoners and cussing each other out. San Patricio will be broke until we get the railroad here. And now, by the gods, this bank robbery has cleaned out what little we did have. Do you blame Tolleston for being mad?"

Webb asked, "And you can't cross over into Wintering to hunt the bank robbers?"

"Not without havin' to fight the whole county," Wardecker said grimly.

Webb settled back into silence, pondering what Wardecker had just told him. He didn't see how he would be included in this fight. He had no share in it, nothing at stake here—only the winning of his freedom. And yet there were some things here he didn't understand, and which he wanted to clear up. Was Tolleston recruiting gun fighters, and would he offer Webb his freedom if he would fight for him? Try as he might, Webb could think of no other reason for Wardecker's saying what he had.

"Look here, Wardecker. What started this row?" Webb asked. "What happened back in Texas?"

Before the sheriff could answer, the door opened and Buck Tolleston entered. He only glanced at Wardecker and went over to Webb.

"I was just talking to Iron Hat Petty," Buck said with deceptive mildness. "He claims you and McWilliams stopped just outside of town for a parley before the bank was held up."

Webb rose and looked down at him, his patience evaporated in an instant. "That's when I got the hand-cuffs, you jug-headed little fool!"

Tolleston smiled meagerly. "It couldn't have been, too, that you was a couple of minutes ahead of time, could it?

It couldn't have been that you stopped to look at your watch and stall for five minutes or so?"

Wardecker heaved himself to his feet and reached for his crutch.

"Buck, will you get the hell out of here?" he asked sternly. "Iron Hat Petty has been so drunk for the last ten years he couldn't see that far. Now get out!"

Tolleston's face was dark with fury, but even he could see that Wardecker had lost his usual mildness and meant exactly what he said. He swallowed once, and without looking at the sheriff, said to Webb, "Come along," and stomped out the door.

Webb looked at Wardecker. "It's mighty easy for a sheriff to lose a prisoner. You the kind that don't care, Wardecker?"

"Nothin'll happen. Only don't fight with him."

"You better gag me, then."

Wardecker grinned. "Maybe that would be better all around. Now go along, Cousins. And don't make trouble. I'll be seein' you soon."

Tolleston was waiting outside. Together they walked down to the O. K. corral. Tolleston left orders for the three Broken Arrow hands in the posse to return to the ranch as soon as they could. From Iron Hat Petty he rented a horse. Webb got a look at Iron Hat, and his anger at the man died.

Iron Hat was old, rheumatic, and moved with a broken-arched gait that was little more than a creep. A bulbous, purple-veined nose was ample testimony to his drinking habits, but for all of that, his bleared eyes were shrewd, his comments, made in a thick, whisky-muted voice, dry and sharp. His derby was green with age, and he wore it squarely on his bald head.

Webb looked over the horse Tolleston hired for him. It was a bay, chunky, big of chest, a stayer.

"I'll send it back tomorrow, Iron Hat," Tolleston said.

"You better trade him," Iron Hat said lazily, indicating Webb.

"Why?"

"If he ever gets out of gun range with his horse you'll play hell catchin' him on that nag of yours."

"What's the matter with my horse?" Tolleston demanded belligerently.

"Nothin'. Only the bay is better. You better trade him."

Tolleston said grimly, "He won't get out of gun range."

"No, but I reckon he'd feel a lot better if you took the best horse. So would I," Iron Hat said. He turned to Webb. "I'll pasture your roan." And he turned and walked away, leaving Tolleston grim-jawed and surly.

Once away from Wagon Mound, riding through a rolling country whose rises were stippled with scrub piñon and cedar, Webb observed the country with the practiced eyes of a cowman. The grama grass was thick and deep, and while many of the arroyos they crossed were dry, a good many more ran water, and lots of it. It was typically good range of the Southwest, with the exception that it had a wealth of water along with its shelter and feed. Far to the north and west, thrusting their jagged peaks to the cavalcade of swollen clouds, lay the Frying Pans. Their lower reaches were black in the distance, indicating full timber, but halfway up their slopes it gave way to gaunt and barren rock, as if the desert beyond were waging a war which had already won it the peaks and half the slopes.

Fat, solid cattle spooked away from them, and once, surprising a cow with her calf as they climbed out of an arroyo, their horses were chased a short way. As the cow stopped, regarding herself the victor, Tolleston smiled, and Webb expected him to comment on the shape of the stuff they had seen.

Instead, Tolleston said, "What brung you into that

gang over in Wintering, Cousins?"

"Hell with you," Webb said calmly.

Tolleston ignored this. He said, "Ever work on a cow outfit?"

"Some."

"Break horses?"

"A few."

"Any job you can't do around an average spread?"

"Cook for money."

"Good," Tolleston said. "I don't reckon you'll have to here."

They did not speak again until late afternoon, when they had forked off three separate wagon roads, each time the trail becoming fainter. Then, topping a rocky rise, Tolleston pulled up and waved off to the north. "That's the Broken Arrow," he said, not without pride.

Before them, at one edge of a deep and wide, grassy valley knifed by a willow-bordered creek, lay the ranch buildings of the Broken Arrow. To Webb, who had traveled through a large part of cattle land, the place spoke to him in his own language. The house itself was a two-story stone affair with a gallery running across the front, and adobe wings branching off on either side. Giant cottonwoods cast their lace umbrellas over it, leaving it deep in shade. Off to the north lay the cluster of sheds and corrals, all solid, all well kept. Between the two lay the long adobe bunk house and cook shack adjoining. All of it had been built for an eye to utility, yet it had achieved a kind of rough beauty that was not all age, and it made Webb look again at Tolleston.

Afterward, riding through the valley and crossing the plank bridge that spanned the creek in front of the house, Webb saw that it held as much as it promised. While all of it had the indolent, mellow air of a home ranch, still the firm hand of discipline could be seen. The harness, the wagons, all the gear that goes to clutter up a corral lot, were in good shape, kept that way by work. It was almost dusk when they turned their horses into the horse corral, slung the saddles over the poles, and turned toward the bunk house.

A cluster of men loafed around its door, and it was for this group that Tolleston headed. The hands fell silent as they approached, and Webb felt their quiet, prying gaze as they observed him.

Tolleston stopped before them and spoke to a sober-faced, middle-aged man who stepped out to meet him.

"Mac, this here is Webb Cousins—the man that held up the bank in town today, along with six other rannies. He's the county's prisoner, but the funds was cleaned out in the robbery, and they've give him to me to guard. You'll work him like you do the rest of the men, but he'll carry no gun, and he'll never ride alone unless with my permission." He turned to Webb. "This is McCaslon, my foreman."

McCaslon looked at Webb briefly, coldly, and said to Tolleston, "Did you say the bank?"

Tolleston told them. Webb watched the faces of the seven men as they listened to their boss, wondering if they, too, shared this common animosity toward the neighboring county. They did. They were utterly motionless, listening closely as the story unfolded. When Tolleston was finished, they looked at each other, and then at Webb. It was McCaslon who looked the longest, and in his eyes Webb could see a hard and relentless dislike shaping up.

McCaslon said, "And he's in with them five and McWilliams?"—indicating Webb.

"That's what I think."

"You want us to lock him up?"

Tolleston hesitated a moment, torn between his desire to be on the safe side and the memory of what Wardecker had said.

"No," he said at last, regarding Webb thoughtfully. "I don't reckon so. When we get proof, there's time enough for that. But I want him kept around the place for the present—or until I tell you."

"Uh-huh," McCaslon said softly, a trace of a hidden promise in the look he gave Webb.

The cook's triangle clanged out into the night then, and Tolleston said, "As soon as you've finished eating, bring him up, Mac," and left.

All the hands turned, waiting for Mac to say something. He did, and said it to Webb. "Go on in." He indicated the cook shack.

The hands made a lane for Webb, and he walked through it into the building, his face faintly amused. The cook shack was not a lot different from most, a long, bare room containing a heavy table almost as long as the room itself, which was flanked by rough benches.

Mac looked around at the men seating themselves. "Where's Stoop?" he asked.

"Out," someone said carelessly.

"Take this place, then," Mac told Webb, indicating the place to his right. Webb obeyed, wondering, and when he was seated he counted the men. Six. There had been seven outside. Webb knew what was coming, for he knew cow-punchers well enough to understand their reasoning. What Tolleston had told them about him called for a court and judgment of their own, and since Tolleston had not expressly forbid them to indulge in their own brand of discipline, they had silently assumed that he did not care.

The food was passed around in silence. Webb helped himself, saying nothing, not even looking up from his plate. He heard a man enter, looked up briefly to observe a gaunt and slouching puncher in the doorway, then turned his attention to his plate.

"Company, Stoop," one of them said, waving a fork

at Webb. Webb looked up. He wanted to remember the man who spoke for he was the one who had started it. He saw a solid, chunky man with a rather full face th̶ suggested a kind of cross-grained innocence. The m̶ was grinning pleasantly enough, but there was a smo̶ ing impudence in his eyes. He had a mischievous ̶ok about him, but maybe that was because of what w̶ ̶ap-pening. Webb looked from him up to the man ̶ had just entered. Webb had seen this man outside ̶t the stranger said, "Why, howdy."

Webb nodded and resumed his eating.

"Buck brought him home," the inn̶ ̶nt-looking puncher continued. "He's a guest of the c̶ ̶."

"A what?"

"Well, prisoner, I reckon. He stuck̶ the bank at Wagon Mound this mornin'. Buck bro̶ ̶t him home to stuff."

"Well, well," Stoop said, elaborately interested. "Ain't no one told him about the private dinin' room?"

"Huh-uh. He was too hungry."

"Reckon I'd better?" Stoop continued, walking around the table.

"I wouldn't know," his partner retorted.

Stoop stopped behind Webb. "All the county guests is fed in the private dinin' room, mister. That there"—he indicated an upended cartridge case in the corner beside a rickety chair—"is it. You'll notice that window beside it is barred. That's because we like to make the county's guests plumb at home."

"A little drafty," Webb drawled, and returned to his food. All the hands, including McCaslon, had stopped eating and were watching Webb.

"He's delicate," the man said. "That's why they wouldn't lock him up in town."

"Well, now," Stoop said mildly. "So am I̶. ̶ ̶ why they ain't locked me up. That's why I don't aim to ̶ the private dinin' room." He paused. "Fella, you're in the wrong pew. Move out!"

"I like it here," Webb said mildly.

Stoop reached out, seized Webb's collar, and yanked back. Webb came out flying, twisted in mid-air, and as soon as his foot was planted behind the bench, arched a tight hook into Stoop's belly. The result was automatic. Stoop folded up like a jackknife, sat down, put both hands across his stomach, and retched audibly for air.

Webb looked around the table and murmured, "The flies are bad in here," and sat down and resumed his eating. No one said a word.

When Stoop stopped his gagging and dragged himself to his feet, Webb turned to him. "Do you like it that way, or with a little salt on it, friend?"

Stoop glared at him a long moment, then said softly, "We ain't finished with each other, fella." He walked to the foot of the table, turned up a plate, and demanded food in a surly tone. Webb looked over at the chunky puncher, who was observing him with curious good humor.

"Pass Stoop the blood," Webb drawled to him. "Take a bucket of it for yourself as it goes by."

The impudent puncher grinned, and it was with friendliness this time. "I'll do that," he said, "and I'll take mine without salt, too."

The meal was finished in silence, and Webb knew that for the present he would be let alone. When he had rolled and lighted a cigarette, McCaslon, who had observed all that went on with the same poker face and eyes which had grown increasingly thoughtful, said, "Come along," and rose.

Webb followed him out into the night.

McCaslon paused out of earshot of the bunkhouse. "That's a good way to get shot in the back."

"I thought of that, too," Webb answered.

"A man with more sense would have taken it a mite slower."

"Now you know that ain't true," Webb said mildly, but positively.

McCaslon turned. "I reckon I do," he said, and started for the house. Ahead of them they saw the front door open and a figure step inside. McCaslon grunted.

CHAPTER FIVE

THEY ENTERED THE OFFICE at the side of the house. It was a small cubbyhole affair holding an untidy desk, a pile of boots and slickers and rifles in inspired disarray.

McCaslon had to shove a stack of magazines out of the way to gain entrance. The far door, opening onto the rest of the house, was open.

McCaslon said, "Wait here," took off his hat, and walked through the far door. Webb could hear voices, one of them a woman's, and it spoke curtly. Presently McCaslon loomed up in the doorway and said, "Come along." His face had an uneasy, harassed look about it.

Webb followed him into a passage which led onto a large room, furnished in a style outmoded years before. All the furniture, Webb guessed, had been freighted out in Conestoga wagons. By the big coal-oil lamp resting on the table in the center of the room Webb could see a girl sitting in a deep leather chair beside the fireplace, which held a bed of red coals. Tolleston was standing over her, and he raised his head to glance at Webb, then returned his gaze to the girl.

"Answer me," he said sharply.

There was no reply. McCaslon cleared his throat.

"We'll wait in the office, Buck."

"You'll wait right here!" Buck said bluntly, and added. "You used to dandle her on your knee, Mac. You've licked her more than once. But she's a little above tellin'

things to people now. Wants privacy." He addressed the
girl mockingly. "Well, you've got it. Now, will you ░
me where you've been?"

The girl rose and stared coolly at Webb and McCas░ ░
She was almost the height of her father, dressed in cl░ ░es
similar to his. Her mass of tawny, wind-blown ha░ ░ay
in a loose knot at the base of her neck. Her full ░ ░th
was set firmly, and there was more than a hint ░ her
father in the line of her jaw. Webb thought she ░ould
smile at McCaslon; she almost did, and then ap░ ░ntly
decided it was no time for it.

"If that's all, dad, I'll go," she said quietly.

Tolleston snorted. "Mrs. Partridge is waiti░ ░n the
kitchen, keepin' your food warm. This is the se░ ░d time
this week she's had to do that."

"How many times has she waited supper for you this
week?" she asked him mockingly.

"What's that got to do with it?" Tolleston snapped.
"When I'm late, it's for a reason. And I can ride this
range in safety because I carry a gun."

The girl was not looking at him now; she was watching Webb, a mixture of friendliness and curiosity in her
voice. She said to Mac, "Did you come in to talk to dad,
Mac?"

Mac nodded. To her father she said, "You might intro-
duce your guest to me, dad, instead of combing me over."

"He's no guest," Tolleston said grimly. "He's a jail-
bird. You ride all over Heaven knows where with trash
like him runnin' loose in the county. For Pete's sake, girl,
can't you see it? And you won't tell me where you go?"

For answer she leaned over and kissed her father, then
left the room, glancing strangely at Webb as she went.

Tolleston growled something in his throat and yanked
out his tobacco sack. He rolled a smoke swiftly, lighted it,
and stood on the hearth, teetering on his heels, looking at
the floor.

McCaslon cleared his throat and Buck looked up, then said, "Oh! Sit down."

It was a long minute before Tolleston spoke, and when he did he talked swiftly to Mac.

"I want a man sent over to this man's country—or what he claims is his country—to check up on his story. Who can you spare?"

Mac thought a moment and said, "Regan, I reckon."

"Go get him. Bring another man along that you can spare for a couple of days, too. Better make it Budrow."

Mac went out and returned with Stoop and the innocent-looking man. Webb did not know which was Regan until Tolleston said, "Listen careful to this, Regan."

"Sure," Stoop said.

Tolleston addressed Webb. "Tell him where this place is you claim to come from. Tell him who you worked for, and for how long; who you claim to know; who your friends claim to be."

Webb told him he came from over in Big Joe County; that he worked for the Double Pitchfork; that he was breaking out horses for Henry Warren; that his friends were almost anyone in the county-seat town who would talk.

When he was finished, Buck said to Stoop, "You got that? All right, get some grub from Charley and light out."

"Tonight?"

"Yes. Now."

Stoop went out. The chunky man fiddled with his Stetson until Tolleston said a little less sharply, "Sit down, Budrow. This'll take time."

Then Tolleston, talking to Budrow, again reviewed the bank robbery in town that morning and the part Webb had played in it. Webb noticed that Tolleston remembered and related everything, even down to Iron Hat Petty's bit of dubious evidence.

"Now, Budrow, what I want you to do is this," Tolleston said. "I want you to ride down to Bull Foot."

McCaslon leaned forward, his mouth open to speak, but Buck did not even glance at him.

"You've never been down there, and to the best of memory, no Wintering man has ever seen you since you've been in this country, has he?"

Budrow scowled. "No, I don't reckon so. I came over the mountains from the west, and this is the first spread I made. It took a couple of months for you feed me up, and I ain't been to Wagon Mound only three, four times."

"Yes. So you won't be known. We'll brand a horse for you so your brand won't give you away. You'll travel tonight and put into Bull Foot tomorrow from the south. I want you to hang around Bull Foot, in the saloons, dance halls, gamblin' layouts, and such. Talk to anyone that'll talk—even the sheriff. And keep your eyes open. What I want is this—any kind of proof you can get that this bank robbery in Wagon Mount was planned by that Wintering crew. I don't care how long it takes. Get a job with an outfit if you have to. If you see anybody spendin' more money than usual, find out where it came from. Be inquisitive, act dumb, get drunk, pick up with saloon bums. Do anything that'll get you this information. And when you get it, ride back to me with it."

McCaslon said slowly, "Buck, that's liable to take a man a year. Is it worth it, just so's you can put a noose on this man's neck?" He jerked a thumb at Webb.

"That isn't all of it, Mac," Tolleston slowly replied. "I like to see justice done, and I aim to see Cousins gets justice. But more than that, I think it'll mean a toe-hold that'll give us a chance to smash that Wintering crowd for good and all."

"How?"

Tolleston's eyes focused on Mac. "How?" he said

gently. "This way. Maybe I got a longer memory than most of you. Maybe I haven't, but it seems like I'm the only man here that can remember the day we picked up and left our range over there in Wintering to start all over again up here. I never forget it. It's with me all the time, Mac—that and the picture of that Bannister outfit hootin' at us from the hills as we drove our stuff off." His voice was grave, measured, more impersonal than Webb had heard it before, and therefore, he guessed, richer in meaning than any other words Tolleston had spoken.

"I remember it, Mac. I live for the day when I'll pay off that score. But I can't do it without men—and haven't got them."

"The whole country remembers it, Buck. All us old timers, anyway."

"But not like me and you," Tolleston said swiftly. "They remember it, but they don't get fightin' mad over it. They've worked up new places here, had families and built up their herds. Men like Will Wardecker, who fought Wake Bannister like a wildcat and had his horse shot out from under him by one of Wake's crew. He was crippled for life by that fall. But does he remember it? Hell, no! He says, 'Let's live in peace.' There's others like him. As long as they're let alone they won't fight." He smiled narrowly now, and in his eyes was the light of a single wild idea. "Now they've lost their money in this bank robbery. They're cleaned out, and they'll be mad." He paused to isolate what he was about to say.

"Then if I can prove that the Wintering outfit—the Bannisters and that crowd of rabble—was behind this hold-up, I'll have what I want. An army—a hog-wild, blood-hungry army. And once I get it on the move, I'll have Bull Foot in ashes and Wintering County only a memory."

Mac sighed and nodded. Webb watched them both, trying to understand the depths of their hatred. He thought he could, for this was a private feud only on a bigger scale, and the success of feuds that left families decimated, a country ravaged, lay in a single man's ability to enlist scores under his banner. But to the injustice of it, the bloody cruelty of its course, Buck Tolleston was blind.

Right now he tried to roll another cigarette, and his fingers were trembling so that he dropped the paper in disgust. Taking a deep breath to steady himself, he said to Budrow:

"That's what I want from you, Budrow. It'll dangerous. If you're caught you're a dead man. They feel kind over having a deputy shot on the doorste our sheriff's office, no matter if the man was a crook a was running with their own bought outlaws. I'd do th myself if I could get away with it, but I can't. And I'm not making you. Do it if you like."

"I'll do it," Budrow said bluntly, and rose.

"Good," Tolleston said briefly. "Sharpen up a knife. I'll be out in a moment and we'll change that Broken Arrow brand to a Double Diamond Bar." To Mac he said, "Give him a hand, Mac." He turned to Webb. "You stay here."

When the other two had gone, Tolleston sat down. He seemed to have forgotten that Webb was in the room, except that occasionally he would turn his head to regard Webb with something like curiosity. Finally he rose and walked over to the hearth and put his back to the now-dead coals.

"That girl was my daughter, Martha," he said apropos of nothing.

Webb did not reply, waiting.

"You told me this afternoon you could do almost any work around a ranch, didn't you?"

Webb nodded.

"And probably like doin' it?"

"That's why I'm punchin' cows and breakin' horses instead of counter jumpin'."

"And you'd rather stick up banks than do either,"
Tolleston said quietly. Webb did not bother to reply to
this.

"Well, since you like to work on a spread, I don't aim
to let you," Tolleston went on calmly. "I've got another
job for you."

When Webb still said nothing, Tolleston went on:
"My girl rides away from the spread two or three times a
week. She's gone all day. I want to know where she goes."

"You want me to spy on her?" Webb asked scornfully.

"Yes. Spy on her," Tolleston echoed, as if he were not
ashamed of the word.

"And if I don't?"

"Mrs. Partridge has a fruit cellar out behind the house.
It hasn't got a window. I've got a pair of leg-irons
around somewhere. Make your choice, and Wardecker be
damned."

"You've made it for me."

"I thought so. And in case you have any fancy notions
about breakin' away from me and headin' out of the
country, I've got another piece of good news."

Webb watched him.

"I fired a man last year for ridin' his horses until he
ruined 'em. I've got a wind-broke sorrel of his out in the
pasture that I aimed to pension. He'll be yours. He can't
travel over a slow trot."

Webb grinned in spite of himself.

"That leaves only one possibility," Tolleston said
slowly. "You might overtake Martha and want her horse.
She wouldn't give him to you. She'd fight." Tolleston
paused. "As crooked a man as you appear to be, I still
don't think you'd hit a woman. And you'd have to if you
got that horse."

"Coming from you, that's almost a compliment, Tolleston," Webb observed.

"It is," Buck agreed bluntly. "Now, give us a hand with this horse outside."

At the horse corral, three riders were just dismounting, talking to Mac and Budrow as they removed the saddles from their tired horses. They were the three Broken Arrow hands who had been in the posse.

Talk ceased as Tolleston and Webb approached.

"Well?" Tolleston demanded.

"Never saw anything but their dust," one of the weary hands said. "They crossed over into Wintering on the road. We followed 'em to the mouth of Wailing Canyon, and then some line rider up on the rim started throwin' shots at us."

"Did you smoke him out?"

"Sure. But they was gone by the time we did."

"Still goin' south?"

"Uh-huh."

Tolleston turned his head and looked steadily at Webb. "Well, well," he said mildly, meaningly.

CHAPTER SIX

Mitch Budrow stopped in Wagon Mound—so named because of the tall butte shaped somewhat like a Conestoga wagon which lay to the west—and passed the time of night with the hostler at the O. K. corral. He wanted to be seen. Then he mounted and rode south out of town, but as soon as he was out of sight he angled west off the road and lifted his horse into a stiff trot. He held this southwesterly course most of the night, so that, had he been observed by a man who knew the country, Mitch's claim that he was heading for Bull Foot would not have been believed. But Mitch would never have claimed it, for he had never intended going there.

It was still night when he crossed the county line. He observed the occasion without a trace of relief or apprehension, for Mitch Budrow held no illusions about the part he was playing. He would probably get it in the back some day, no matter what county he happened to be riding through, and he reflected without rancor that, although there are strange ways of paying back debts, this was the strangest.

The grass of the small prairie he was crossing was lush, and he could hear the swish of its dew-laden richness against his horse's legs. He was not sure of his trail, since he had made this trip at night only five times in twice that many months, but once he felt his horse slope steeply down the side of the swale he looked around him

at the starshot blackness, almost certain. And when his
horse crossed a stream he was sure, and he turned down
it, at ease. If his guess was right, this was Copperstone
Creek, and he had only to follow its rather direct course
to arrive at Wake Bannister's home ranch. Ever since he
crossed the county line he had been riding on Bannister's Dollar range, and if he were to ride till the next
sunset in the same direction, he would still be on it.
Mitch gave little thought to this, however; better men
than himself had accepted the name of Bannister as
meaning bigness and power and wealth.

It was one of these big Bannister men that Mitch was
thinking of, and trying not to. By the time the first faint
shafts of the sun cut straight across the earth, bringing
every blade of grass into momentary relief, Mitch kne
what he was going to say. He lifted his gaze across   .e
vast hollow ahead of and below him, and he saw that the
sun had not yet touched the Dollar spread. But even in
this muted light he could see its size, and he marveled
quietly.

Like many a western ranch, it lay on the banks of a
creek. But this was not a ranch in the accepted sense of
the word; it was almost a town. The big main house,
which dominated the rest of the place through the simple
fact that it had appropriated all the largest trees, was
still a little strange to Mitch. He had never seen a tenth
of its rooms, and he knew he never would. Being a dry-
country man, used to adobe and stone and maybe a log
shack in the high line camps, Mitch never got over his
initial awe of seeing a whole vast two-story building made
of thick, unspliced logs. So were its wings, and so were
their wings. The whole affair angled and turned, doubled
back until it seemed to Mitch that all the forests in all the
mountains must have been cut to supply material.

The barns and sheds, a good way from the house, were
of stone, more familiar, and the huge and rambling com-

bination bunk house and cook shack was of adobe that
matched the huddle of houses behind it, in which the
Mexican field hands lived. All of this, with the exception
of the corrals, contrived to sprawl around a bare plaza,
where the ranch store thrust up its tin roof behind its
false front.

By full sun-up, when the place came alive, Mitch had
put up his horse in the small corral behind the store, as
he had been ordered to do, and made his way to the main
house. At a door in one of the wings close to the black
smith shop he paused. There was a tangle of scrap iron
and wheel rims to the side of the door, and Mitch surveyed it with the mild disapproval of an orderly man.

He looked up to behold the blacksmith in his under
shirt sleeves watching him from the wide door of the
shop.

"Morning," the blacksmith said.

"Morning," Mitch replied, and said no more. He had
been ordered not to. He let himself into the room which
was Wake Bannister's office and the nerve center of the
Dollar spread. It was big, bare of furniture except for a
rickety desk and a half dozen sorry-looking chairs. Mitch
sat in one of them and rolled a smoke, and let the hot,
stale air of the room take the chill off him.

He was almost drowsing when the door opened to
admit first a tuneful whistle and then a man. Mitch was
on his feet when the man entered.

Wake Bannister had been called many things in his
fifty years, but he had never been called ineffectual. To
begin with, his presence was awesome. Six foot six—mas-
sive-shouldered, white-haired, lazy as a cat, there was
something almost electric in his being. Men felt it when
they talked to him, felt it almost as much as they felt the
sharp, piercing blue of his eyes. His face, while weather-
burned and sun-wrinkled, had never mellowed, never
softened. It combined the aggressive jaw with the think-

er's broad forehead, a contradiction which was the key to
the man. His nose was thin, and the whitest part of his
face was where the skin drew tight over its high bridge.

Right now he caught sight of the waiting Mitch, and
he paused in his stride, his whistle dying.

"I thought I told you not to come here unless you had
something to say," he said mildly. He had a fine voice,
too, soft and low and penetrant, but maybe this was because men stopped talking when he opened his mouth.

Mitch shifted to his other foot. "I have."

"About that bank hold-up? I've known it for hours."

"But not all of it," Mitch said.

Bannister regarded him a moment, frowning, then said,
"Pull up a chair. I haven't smoked yet." He sat down at
the desk and offered Mitch a cigar, which was declined,
then lighted one himself.

"What's up?" he asked finally.

Mitch, more at ease now, told Bannister of Tolleston's
conviction that Webb was implicated in the bank stick-
up, along with McWilliams.

"The damn fool," Bannister said quietly. "Go on."

"This Cousins is Tolleston's prisoner now. He has
him over at the Broken Arrow. Tolleston aims to hold
him until he gets proof that Cousins was in on the hold-
up."

Bannister was on the track of something. Mitch knew
he could skip whole sentences now and Bannister would
still follow his meaning.

"That's why I'm here. Tolleston told me to head for
Bull Foot and stay there until I got some kind of proof
that the five robbers were hired by this county. That
would tie up McWilliams with them, and Cousins, too."

"You didn't come here to tell me Buck is trying to
frame a saddle bum." Bannister said instantly.

"No. Here it is: If Tolleston gets proof that Wintering
County was behind the hold-up, he aims to use it as a pry.

With that pry he'll raise all the ranchers in San Patricio County out of their seats fightin' mad, and when he
has 'em fightin' mad he aims to raid Bull Foot. Burn it
down, plunder the county. He's been waitin' for this,
dreamin' of it—"

"I know," Bannister cut in quietly. He smoked in silence, Mitch watching him.

"Had breakfast?" Bannister asked finally.

"No."

"Go get it and come back."

Mitch rose, Bannister with him. As Mitch was going
out, Bannister said, "I take back what I first said to you.
You've got judgment, boy."

Mitch flushed with pleasure. "Anyone could've seen
you'd want to know that."

"Why?" Bannister asked curiously.

Mitch was tripped up. His answer would sound pretty
obvious, but it was the only one he could think of. "Why,
so you'll be ready to meet him."

Bannister murmured, "Oh, hell," and turned away.
"Come back after you've eaten. Maybe your head'll be
clearer."

After Mitch had gone, Bannister cocked his booted feet
up on the desk and smoked. The blacksmith across the
way had started work, and the ring of his sledge, bell
clear, true, rhythmical, gave Bannister a feeling of real
pleasure. He liked to hear it around him hour after hour.

Whenever he had a spare moment, Bannister would
go over to old Symonds's shop and watch him. Sometimes he would help Symonds, and these times he would
be ordered around like any fumble-fingered apprentice.
He took his cursings, always deserved, and sweated away,
trying to recover his mistakes. He and Symonds never
talked, but Bannister respected him more than any man
he knew. He listened now to the *slam, tap-tap; slam, tap-
tap,* and could almost picture the iron's white glow and

Symonds tentative blows before the heavy sledging once started. He wanted to go over and watch, but he fought the impulse. Instead, he walked to the door and stood in , observing Symonds.

When the blacksmith looked up, Bannister said gravely, "Mornin', Symonds."

"Mornin'," Symonds answered.

"Hit the gong," Bannister said, and went inside. The lash of a heavy triangle boomed out over the morning air. It was Bannister's way of calling his foreman.

Hugo Meeker was ten minutes in coming. He d   ot apologize for his lateness; it was understood by them   th that some jobs could not be left. Meeker had come .   n Texas with Bannister, but his appearance had hanged in the last twenty-five years. His wedgelike ja leak eyes, his languorous movements, his rare smile, h hard, driving speech, were the same now as always. H body was leaner, perhaps, saddle gaunt, and he smoked more, but they were the only differences.

Sitting down in the chair Mitch had just vacated, Hugo waited until Bannister quit looking out the window and dropped his cigar butt on the floor.

"You were late last night," Bannister observed.

"Sure," Hugo drawled. "I had a little business that almost got by me."

He reached in his hip pocket and took out an already opened letter. It was addressed to Wake Bannister.

"That come in the mail last night for you. I had a hunch and opened it."

Bannister looked at the letterhead on the envelope, which read *Southwestern Railroad*. Taking out the letter, he unfolded and read it, and his eyes glinted with a kind of simmering excitement.

"So they're building on through to Wagon Mound," he said softly, looking at Hugo. "Advance agents comin' in a month. Well?"

"I had another hunch," Hugo drawled. He reached in his shirt pocket this time and took out a letter addressed to Sheriff William Wardecker, Wagon Mound. It bore the same letterhead. Bannister opened it and read. It contained the brief news that the railroad was building through to Wagon Mound, and that their advance agent would be in San Patricio County within a month to arrange for the purchase of right of way.

"Well?" Bannister asked again.

"The Wagon Mound stage was just loading at the depot. As soon as I read your letter I figured there'd be another like it in the Wagon Mound mail. So I highed it to the ford and got the letter."

"Held up the stage, you mean?"

Hugo nodded. "I was quiet as a kitten. I took the sack, waved the stage on, built a fire, found the letter I wanted, and then took the cut over the mesa, held up the stage again and give them back their mail." He was laughing silently. "They'll have a hard time figurin' that one out."

Bannister smiled fondly at the drawling, insolent indifference of the man. Years ago Wake Bannister had learned this man by heart, or enough of him to know that he thought ahead of ninety men out of a hundred, and could outtalk, fist-whip, or gunfight, and beat the other ten. That was why Hugo Meeker could open Bannister's mail on occasions and never be given the hint of reprimand.

"But we can't keep it quiet long," Hugo drawled. "I've already greased Kean at the telegraph office, so he'll hand over anything sent to Wardecker. But when the railroad don't get an answer, they're liable to write to Tolleston or Patton or even—"

"He's dead."

"Well, any big auger over there."

Bannister nodded absently and picked up the railroad's letter addressed to him and read it again while Meeker rolled a smoke.

"About these horses they want for grading teams," Bannister said. "How soon can we have enough broke out?"

"In a week, if we have to."

"We don't. I'll write and tell them that my boys are out on a drive now, and that it'll take at least a month and a half to break out that many. That won't hurry up things any."

"How much time have we got?"

Bannister looked at his letter. "A little over three weeks, accordin' to this."

"That time enough?"

Meeker settled down in his chair and inhaled deeply on his cigarette. He did not take it out of his mouth when he exhaled, so that a cloud of blue enveloped his face.

"That's cuttin' it close, Wake."

"I don't think so," Bannister said. "Mitch Budrow dropped in this morning."

"I saw his horse back of Mooney's."

"Tolleston suspects we were behind the hold-up. So we're saved the trouble of puttin' the suspicion in their minds over there."

Meeker said softly, "The hell he does? What did those boys do—ride Dollar-branded horses?"

Bannister laughed and said, "No. It seems that McWilliams, who was bringing a prisoner back, had lost so much sleep that he couldn't make Bull Foot, so he pulled into Wagon Mound and was going to ask to borrow their jail. He walked right into the hold-up. Tolleston, who is always ready to blame Wintering for anything, claimed McWilliams and his prisoner were part of the gang."

"Who was the prisoner?" Meeker asked.

"A saddle bum name of Webb Cousins. Wanted for that train stick-up last year."

"So what does Tolleston do now?"

"I had another hunch," Hugo drawled. He reached in his shirt pocket this time and took out a letter addressed to Sheriff William Wardecker, Wagon Mound. It bore the same letterhead. Bannister opened it and read. I contained the brief news that the railroad was buildin through to Wagon Mound, and that their advance agent would be in San Patricio County within a month to a range for the purchase of right of way.

"Well?" Bannister asked again.

"The Wagon Mound stage was just loading at th depot. As soon as I read your letter I figured there'd b another like it in the Wagon Mound mail. So I high tailed it to the ford and got the letter."

"Held up the stage, you mean?"

Hugo nodded. "I was quiet as a kitten. I took the sack waved the stage on, built a fire, found the letter I wante and then took the cut over the mesa, held up the stage again and give them back their mail." He was laughing silently. "They'll have a hard time figurin' that one out."

Bannister smiled fondly at the drawling, insolent indifference of the man. Years ago Wake Bannister had learned this man by heart, or enough of him to know that he thought ahead of ninety men out of a hundred, and could outtalk, fist-whip, or gunfight, and beat the other ten. That was why Hugo Meeker could open Bannister's mail on occasions and never be given the hint of reprimand.

"But we can't keep it quiet long," Hugo drawled. "I've already greased Kean at the telegraph office, so he'll hand over anything sent to Wardecker. But when the railroad don't get an answer, they're liable to write to Tolleston or Patton or even—"

"He's dead."

"Well, any big auger over there."

Bannister nodded absently and picked up the railroad's letter addressed to him and read it again while Meeker

Bannister nodded, and Meeker went out. Mitch was waiting outside and stepped in at Meeker's invitation. He sat in the same chair and held his Stetson in his blunt hands, his attitude much like an atte ive pupil.

Bannister said mildly, "Tonight y t back to Tolleston and tell him that you saw two of g Montana hardcases drinking in a back room of s Melodian with Hugo Meeker today."

Mitch nodded.

"That's all," Bannister said. "Go on he store and tell Mooney to give you his back n and sleep till dark." He looked at Mitch thoughtfu "Any curiosity?" he asked.

Mitch quickly shook his head. There wa ne of the old impudence in his eyes.

"When you come back next time, I want s ow when Tolleston is planning to raid Bull Foot, w oute he aims to travel, how many men he aims to brn along, and who they are. Can you do it?"

Mitch nodded. "Mac will know, and he'll talk to me. I'll get word to you."

"All right." Bannister turned away. "I'm sending your mother a check for a thousand dollars tonight."

Mitch's eyes looked uneasy. "Thanks," he said, then: "How is she?"

"She started a little store with that last check I sent." He smiled meagerly. "Each letter she wants to know more about her boy who died a hero saving my trail herd from rustlers."

Mitch flushed. "I'm obliged, sir. I'd rather have her think that than know the truth."

"I daresay she'd prefer it, too," Bannister said dryly. "By the way, that U. S. marshal from Tucson is still corresponding with me over you. The woman's murder has never been solved—naturally. It seems he'd heard you were headed for this basin."

Mitch waited humbly.

"I'm having a hard time convincing him he's wrong."

Mitch's eyes were filled with a gratitude that Bannister had seen only in dogs, and he turned away in disgust. He couldn't help hating weak men. Even a woman killer was less despicable if he retained his spirit and pride. But ever since the day Hugo Meeker had found Mitch Budrow gaunt and starved and sick and delirious in his mean fugitive's camp up over the Frying Pans, Bannister had never seen him show spirit. He had gladly consented to act as a spy in Tolleston's home ranch; had even shown an amazing resourcefulness when he wandered into a Broken Arrow line camp and collapsed. He had been taken by Tolleston's hands to the home ranch, and in time had easily found a place there. More than once he had given Bannister valuable information, but Bannister despised him. He even despised the petty blackmail necessary to insure Mitch's loyalty.

He was barely civil now. "Come back when you've got what I asked."

Mitch left quietly, cowed to the very core of him.

In a few minutes Bannister rose and went over to the blacksmith shop. He said to Symonds, "Some of the boys will be bringing their ponies in for shoeing, Symonds. I want you to look their feet over carefully."

"Startin' when?"

"This morning."

To Symonds this meant only one thing. There would be considerable riding on rock. And the only considerable expanse of rock around these parts lay over in San Patricio County.

"All right," he said. It was none of his business.

CHAPTER SEVEN

TOLLESTON HAD HIS HORSE SADDLED by the time hands were finished breakfast. He stopped Mac and Bob, and told Webb his duties; they were all simple petty, all pointedly trivial, designed to keep him within sight of the house. While two of the hands cut and hauled cedar poles from the hills, Webb was to set the anchor posts for a new corral. He was to clean the old feed corral, then patch the roof on the cookshack, then do some needed blacksmithing on wagon tires. All the jobs, Tolleston had emphasized, would place him in clear view of the horse corral, where Martha Tolleston's pony was. If Webb saw her take her horse out, he was to take the blaze-face sorrel from the corral and follow her. With these instructions given, Tolleston left for town, and Webb set about work under Mac's watchful eye.

In mid-afternoon, as he was pitching dirt on the bunkhouse roof, he saw Martha Tolleston leave the house. She was dressed in an outfit of deep brown, a divided skirt, blouse to match, man's Stetson, and boots. He waited until she had saddled her horse and ridden off west, then went over and threw his loop over the sorrel, Mac coming to watch. The horse was docile, and even though he had been on grass for months, did not offer a show of spirit.

Saddling him, Webb was angry at the man who had ruined him, for the horse had lines that argued speed and bottom and fight.

Once out of sight of the house, Webb reined up and considered. Right now, for the first time, he was free of Mac's prying watchfulness. He had a poor horse under him. He had no canteen, no gun, no food. He was re membering everything that Wardecker had told hi about the trouble of getting out of this country. To h with Wardecker. He would try it.

North looked best, the mountains lowest. He wou try it there.

He lifted his horse into a lope, but inside of a mi knew he would have to ease up. The horse was blowing hard. Then, to make up for his slow time, he headed fo the closest rock he could see. Here, at any rate, they woul have a hard time trailing him. He had not been on h way twenty minutes, when he looked back. He saw a ride following him, stopping occasionally to pick up h track.

Webb spurred his horse on, cursing. In another quarter mile, he had to stop. The horse was heaving violently, useless to him as a mount.

Cursing bitterly, Webb waited. Presently the rider came into sight. It was Mac. He rode up to the waiting Webb and pulled up.

"I figured you'd try that. You don't believe a rock's hard till you butt your head against it, eh?"

Webb grinned suddenly. "You can't shoot a man for tryin'."

"Can't I?" Mac said grimly. "I can and I will." He gestured to Webb's horse. "It'll take that nag just nine hours to make the closest foothills. I know, because I've tried her. If you're gone more than three hours this afternoon, I aim to come after you. And next time I do," he said quietly, grimly, "you won't like the place you end up in." He motioned with his arm. "Now git back there and pick up her trail. And remember what I told you."

Webb wheeled his horse and rode back, Mac a dozen

ces behind him. When he came to the tracks of Mar-
a's horse, he turned and followed them. Mac did not
en bother to watch him go. The cocksureness of the
an made Webb angry. He felt like a small child who
as been told what he can and cannot do, ar   o gets
aught the first time he makes a misstep.

Grudgingly, then, he turned his attention to   ness.
He would have a better chance of not being se   he
ook the direction in which Martha was traveling   n
ircled wide of it and came back every mile or so to
t up again. Traveling this way, he began to think ab
Martha Tolleston. Buck had never said it, but Webb w
certain that he suspected her of meeting a man. And
Webb found himself anxious to see the man she was
afraid for her father to meet.

At every rise he dismounted and scanned the country
ahead for a sign of the girl, keeping hidden himself. He
was entering more broken country now, a land of shallow
canyons and rock and sandstone rubble and clay, eroded
by wind and water.

Her tracks, when he next picked them up, turned more
to the north, where the land sloped up to a bench and the
canyons were deeper. Webb went cautiously now, for she
was traveling the bed of a crooked arroyo, and the next
bend he rounded, he might stumble upon her.

Where he saw this arroyo fork into a larger one, he
pulled up. Whoever would meet her would doubtless
come up this arroyo, since this would be the only comfort-
able travel here, and if two sets of tracks should be seen
in the sand, there was a chance he might be discovered.

Backtracking a quarter of a mile, he dismounted, left
his horse where it was off the trail and screened by brush,
and set off on foot. Once on the bank of the arroyo, he
traveled it carefully, keeping hidden. He had walked less
than three hundred yards when he saw below him the girl
seated on a rock close to the far bank of the arroyo. Her

horse was ground-haltered in the shade, and she seem
to be waiting for someone.

Webb thought of what Buck Tolleston had said ab
taking her horse. Of course she would fight—or wou
she now?

If he were to go down and say, "Miss Tolleston, yo
old man is havin' me spy on you. I don't want to.
you'll give me your horse, I'll ride off and never both
you again," would she do it? He didn't know, but he w
willing to try.

He was just ready to hoist himself out of the brus
when he heard a whistle far down the arroyo. That woul
be the man she was going to meet. Webb sank back, dis
gusted. He knew she would not give him her horse on
he had seen the man she was meeting. And then it o
curred to Webb that, if he were close to where she was
he might contrive to steal one of their horses.

He backed away, traveled up the arroyo a few hun
dred yards, crossed it, and came down the far bank. His
approach to the spot where Martha was sitting was careful, quiet, and in the last fifty yards of it, which he
crawled on his hands and knees, he heard the whistle
again, and this time closer. At last he settled himself behind a thick clump of mesquite on the arroyo's rim. Here,
he figured, he could hear enough to know if they strolled
away from the horses or not.

Presently Webb heard the soft *hush, hush* of a horse
traveling in sand. Then he heard a man's voice call out,
"Hello, Marty."

For some unaccountable reason, Webb disliked the
voice the minute he heard it. Martha answered quietly,
"Hello, Britt."

"Been waiting long?"

"Not long."

A pause as saddle leather creaked. "The reason I was
late is that I think the old man's having me followed. I

doubled back and waited today."

"Was he?"

"Not today."

Another pause, and then Martha said swiftly, "Please don't, Britt. You've been nice. Don't get sticky."

The man laughed shortly. "If I haven't it hasn't been because I never wanted to, Marty. You know how I've felt about you."

There was a long pause then, and then Martha said quietly, "I know."

"And you've never returned it?"

"How could I, Britt?" Her voice was almost hard with bitterness. "What chance have I had to know you, to see how you live, what it would be like to be together, who your friends are—oh, everything! We've met only when we could sneak away, and then we almost talk in whispers for fear of being overheard. I hate it, Britt!"

"You know how we can fix that, Marty. Get your horse and we'll ride down to Bull Foot and be married by to-morrow morning."

Marty laughed shortly. "Do you think your father would let it stand that way? Do you think mine would?"

"I don't reckon they'd have much to say about it."

"Don't you? Well, I do. I know them—both of them. They'd rather see us dead than have a Tolleston married to a Bannister."

Webb's jaw sagged in surprise. The man Martha was meeting was Britt Bannister of the family that was anathema to Buck Tolleston!

But Martha went on. "No, Britt. T⋯⋯ won't settle it. Before we could ever have any peace t⋯⋯ this sense-less feud has to be settled. We couldn't pr⋯ ⋯d leave what we've grown up with, and still be happy. ⋯ ⋯kele-ton is too big to lock in any closet."

"The world's big, Marty," Britt said. "We could ⋯ ⋯"

"But some day my father is going to kill yours, or yours

is going to kill mine! How would we feel then?"

Britt said nothing.

"And instead of feeling better, I think it's gettin[g]
worse."

"How do you mean?" Britt asked quickly.

"Remember our promise. We were never to tell secret[s]
never to be disloyal." She hesitated. "But haven't you n[o]
ticed it, Britt?"

"Maybe I have, now that you mention it," Britt sai[d]
slowly. "Let me think back."

Webb wanted to see this man, and determined to. Taking off his Stetson, he inched his way forward, hugging
the ground, until his head was at the very edge of the
arroyo bank. Then slowly he raised himself on his elbows
and peered over the edge.

There, sitting on the ground beside Martha, was a man
about Webb's age. His hat lay in the sand beside him, so
that Webb could get a glimpse of his face. Below sleek
black hair his face was much the same as his father's, although Webb did not know that. His eyes were the same
blue, without the chill in them, and the nose was as fine
and sharp. Only the chin was a little less firm, and his
smile was much more ready.

"Remember the time we first met, Britt," Martha said.
"You were eight and I—"

She never finished, for the bank on which Webb was
resting caved in with a gentle rumble and Webb, still on
his belly, coasted down the bank and pulled up at the
bottom in a fog of dust. He looked up to find himself
staring into the gun of Britt Bannister.

Picking himself up, Webb murmured, "Now I might
have known that," and grinned. Martha stood beside
Britt, and the surprise was just washing out of her face,
giving way to anger.

"And just who are you?" Britt asked coldly.

Webb jerked his head toward Martha. "She'll tell you."

"He's a county prisoner dad brought home last night.
think he was implicated in the Wagon Mound hold-up."
Britt's eyes changed a little.

"Escaping? After a horse?"

"I got one, thanks," Webb said, still grinning. "No.
his was the first job Tolleston set me to."

"What?"

"This."

"Eavesdropping?" Martha asked.

"I think your dad called it spying."

Britt's glance swiveled to Martha, but his gun remained cocked, steady, more than a leap away from
Webb.

"Is that straight?" Britt asked her.

"It could be," Martha answered coldly. "I hadn't told
you yet, but he questioned me again last night." She said
to Webb, "What did he tell you to do?"

"He wanted to know where you went—wanted me to
spy on you."

"You overheard everything?"

Webb nodded, and he felt the blood crawling up to
his face. "I climbed up there because I figured you might
leave your horses. I—I aimed to steal one and high-tail it.
Your dad gave me a windbroke horse and I can't escape
on it." He grinned a little as he spoke. "You see, I never
held up the bank. I don't know anything about it—except
that I'd like to get out of here."

Martha said, "And you expect me to give you mine?"

"I'd sure be obliged," Webb said earnestly. "I'd give
you mine. He'd take you back."

Martha's lip lifted in contempt. "You think I'd betray
my father that way?"

Webb shook his head. "No, I didn't reckon you would.
I just wanted to make sure."

Martha said nothing for a moment, then asked Webb,
"You know this is Britt Bannister—the son of the man

dad has sworn to kill"

Webb nodded.

"And if he finds out,   know what will happen?"

"I can guess," Webb s

"Are you going to tell

Webb grinned. "Not a   . If you'll give me you horse, I'll never see him aga

"And if I won't, will you   ack and tell him?"

Webb shook his head. "I re   not. It doesn't interes me."

"That's a lie," Bannister said   ply. "Buck Tolleston would free you for this informat   -he'd give anythin to know it! And I reckon you kn   that!"

"He wouldn't, Britt!" Martha   id quickly. "He wouldn't free a bank robber!"

"That wouldn't matter to Buck," Britt cut in. "I'm trying to think of what would happen to you if he was told, Marty."

Martha's eyes flashed, and her mouth was open for a hot retort when Britt said to Webb, "I know how I'll take care of you, mister."

Reaching for his sack of Durham, Webb shrugged. "I reckon I do, too," Silently Webb was wondering if Britt Bannister knew there was a warrant out for Webb in Wintering County.

He was sure Martha knew it. What Bannister was about to say, Webb guessed, was that he would take Webb over into Wintering County. And once there, Webb knew, it would be discovered that the law wanted him. But if he could bluff it out, he intended to.

So he said, looking at Martha, hoping against hope that she would understand and keep his secret, "Haze me out of the country. That's what you mean, don't you?"

"No," Britt said. "You'll come home with me."

Martha looked at Webb, and he returned her look, his face impassive, waiting. She must have understood, for he heard her say, "Oh, no. Britt. You can't do that

"Why not? If he goes back to the Broken Arrow,
ell your dad."

"But you can't take him with you!" Martha
vehemently.

Britt looked strangely at her. "Why not?"

Martha's glance at Webb seemed to say: *What can I
do?* She turned to Britt. "What will you do w   him?
Keep him locked up for a year?"

"It's been done," Britt said stubbornly.

"But that's cruel, Britt!"

"Would you rather have your dad find out?"

Martha did not know what to do. She look   at Webb
appealingly, and Webb said calmly, "Tell   ."

Britt's look was puzzled. Martha sighed. "All right,
Britt. Haven't you heard, or don't you remember, that
this is the prisoner McWilliams brought into Wagon
Mound—a prisoner of Wintering County? He's wanted
for train robbery in your county, and they'll arrest him
as soon as you take him back."

"So much the better," Britt said, smiling a little. "It'll
save us keeping him locked up."

"But you can't do that, Britt!"

Britt scowled. "What is this? Are you tryin' to defend
a man who's pulled off two robberies?"

"I don't believe it!" Martha said. "I don't"— She hesitated, blushing a little, and then blurted out: "Anyway, I
would hate myself if I sent a man to jail."

"If he's guilty?"

"I'm not," Webb put in. "I happened to be riding the
train, and when your law couldn't find the robbers, they
claimed it was an inside job. There was a tinhorn gam-
bler I knew ridin' that same train, and to work off an
old grudge, I reckon he gave the law my name."

"See?" Martha said.

Britt looked more puzzled than ever. "Are you takin'

the word of a saddle tramp against county officers, Marty?"

Martha said flatly, "I don't believe it, Britt. Anyon[e] could see he wouldn't hold up a train—or a bank, for th[at] matter."

"Your dad thought so."

"I still don't care. Anyway, dad didn't have him locked up."

Britt smiled meagerly. "No. He brought him out so h[e] could do this dirty work for him."

Martha winced, but she was not through fighting. "You know that's not true, Britt. But even if it was, it wouldn'[t] change matters. I'm not going to send this man to jail fo[r] something he never did, just because he was obeying dad's orders."

Britt said patiently, "All right, suppose you think of somewhere we can put him where he won't talk to your dad."

"But he's said he wouldn't!"

Bannister laughed shortly. "Be sensible, girl. What are we to him? Why wouldn't he trade what he knows if it meant freedom." He looked coldly at Webb. "I've listened to enough of this. I'm thinkin' of you, Marty, when I say he has to be put somewhere where he won't talk."

"You could always shoot me," Webb drawled. Immediately, he was sorry he said it, but he was fed up with being discussed and disposed of like a muley steer. And the look Martha gave him seemed to suggest that he was using a poor coin with which to pay her back for siding in with him.

"Well?" Britt said to her.

"I don't know. If you're going to, you're going to, Britt." Then she said, "Could you take him with you— and still not turn him over to the law?"

"Dad's the law in Wintering County," Bannister said. "And he doesn't interfere much with me. Yes, I could take him home, and he wouldn't be turned over to the sheriff."

"Is that your promise, Britt?"

"It's my word."

Martha turned to Webb. "I'm sorry. If—if we knew more about you—or if what we do know didn't look so bad—we could take your word."

"That's right," Webb said dryly. "I got a bad record— accordin' to all the big augers around here who believed somebody else, who believed a crooked tinhorn."

Britt cut in coldly, "Where's your horse?"

Webb told him. Walking down the arroyo with Britt and Martha riding close behind him, Webb raged inside himself. From now on, he swore, there was going to be more scrapping and less submission on his part. If Britt Bannister ever slacked his attention once, from now on, Webb would slug him, take his horse, and jump the country—and the reward posters be damned. He wondered if Britt would go back on his word to the girl and turn him over to the Wintering law. But he did not understand why Martha Tolleston had taken his part, insisting that Britt not give him over to arrest. The only reason he could find was that Buck Tolleston had confided his doubts as to Webb's guilt to her. And this didn't seem right.

At Webb's horse, Britt dismounted, and, while Martha held the gun on Webb, Britt tied his ankles together beneath the sorrel's belly. Webb regarded her with curiosity as she stood before him, and she avoided looking at him.

When all was ready, Britt said to Martha, "Your dad will send out men, after they miss this man, won't he?"

Martha nodded.

"Then hold tight and say nothin'. Let them think what they want. The one thing that'll work for you, Marty, is that you've still got your own horse. So they can't prove you talked to this man, or he'd have taken it away from you."

Martha nodded and they rode off, Webb ahead. He was headed for a new kind of prison—and in the very camp of the Bannisters.

CHAPTER EIGHT

IT HAD BEEN DARK ⟨...⟩ HOURS when Britt and Webb pulled into the Dollar ⟨...⟩ead. Instead of approaching it from the north, as wo⟨...⟩ have been natural, Britt cir-⟨c⟩led around to the west, ⟨...⟩ that he would first go through Mex-town—the district w⟨h⟩ere the adobes of the field hands lay huddled. Webb regarded the place with won-der. Seeing all the lights below, he thought they were about to enter a town. But as they approached, he could see the barns, the corrals, the bulk of the huge house, and now he understood a little more of what Wardecker had told him of Bannister.

Britt, meanwhile, was having a prolonged argument with his conscience. It would be so much easier to turn this redhead over to the sheriff in Bull Foot tomorrow, and get him out of the way for good. But he had prom-ised Martha he would not. Of course, a man could be held here on the Dollar indefinitely; it had been done before. A man doesn't walk or ride away from a place where more than a hundred people are watching him night and day. But this was no ordinary case.

Suddenly Britt decided to play the hunch he had had from the first, and which had led him to enter Mex-town first. Those five hardcases from the north country were putting up in the old bunk house. Not knowing or car-ing about the Wagon Mound robbery, Britt saw nothing strange in their being there; Wake Bannister always seemed to have a mysterious bunch of strangers around him, usually tough. These would be the men that would guard this man for him.

The old bunk house—in use when Bannister first took over this place and designed to house the dozen vaqueros which had since been replaced by white hands—lay just behind the Mexican *cantina*. It had come to be regarded as the place to put up those men whom Bannister did not invite to the main house. Britt ordered Webb past the *cantina*, and they reined up in front of the long, single story stone building.

A man was lounging in the door, a light to his back and he observed the two men in silence.

"Give me a hand here, will you?" Britt asked him.

The man came out beside Britt's horse.

"Put a gun on that man while I untie him."

The man complied with a grunt, and Webb was freed, then told to dismount.

"Into the bunk house," Britt told him.

The three Montana men playing poker with a Mexican looked up as Webb stepped in. They looked at him a long moment, and finally one of them, the oldest, apparently, said from around a match in the corner of his mouth, "Well, well. They still swarmin' over you, son?"

Webb smiled faintly. It was the man who had asked him during the bank hold-up if he wanted the cuffs off. The significance of their presence here was not lost on Webb. Wintering County—or perhaps Bannister—had been behind the hold-up after all, and Tolleston's hunch, based as it was on a false premise, was nevertheless correct.

Britt looked sharply at this man. "You know him?"

"Seen him."

"Where?"

"He was handcuffed to a tin star the last I seen. Over in Wagon Mound."

Another Montana man looked at Webb and said, "The hell he was. I don't remember that, Lute."

"Sure. I offered to turn him loose, but he was bein' a good boy that day."

"He's goin' to be from now on," Britt said, and added generally to the room, "How you fixed for money, boys?"

They looked at each other. The younger Montana man laughed and looked at the man with the match in his mouth. "You tell 'im, Lute."

Lute grinned sheepishly. "Why, last night I was pr[e]tt [w]ell fixed. I ain't now."

"I am," the younger man said, and laughed again, f[inger]ng his stack of chips.

"Then you want to make some?" Britt asked.

"Sure. How easy is it?" Lute asked.

"Plenty. I want this man guarded day and night [and I] don't ever want him out of sight of one of you. If [he] makes a break—let him have it. Understand?"

Lute looked speculatively at Webb. "Play poker, so[n?]" Webb nodded.

"All right," Lute said. "I don't reckon he'll be out of this chair much."

"What about the rest of you?" Britt asked.

They all nodded or said "Yes," and Britt pulled out a wallet and emptied it of gold coins, which spilled all over the table. The noise woke the other two Montana men, who were sleeping in their bunks.

"That much every week," Britt said, and he told the others his proposition.

Lute looked carelessly at the money. "What's the catch in this, Bannister?"

"So long as he stays here, there's none. If he gets away, there'll be plenty," Britt said slowly. It was the kind of speech his father would have made.

There was a movement in the door and Britt turned to behold Hugo Meeker lounging in the doorway.

"Evenin', gents," Hugo drawled, and they answered him. "The old man'd like to see you when you got a minute to spare, Britt."

"All right."

Hugo left, and Britt resumed his business. "I don't know how hard you boys are drinkin', but it won't be an excuse. You better understand that."

Lute put in mildly, "You don't want him to run of All right, he won't."

Britt turned and went out. Walking across the plaz leading the two horses, he thought he could understa why his father liked to use men like those five. They di not ask questions, they understood, and they acted. A they needed was a little money.

He turned his horses over to the horse wrangler at th main corral with instructions that the Broken Arrow horse be turned loose at the county line tomorrow. Then he headed for the wing of the house where Bannister's office was. In spite of the fact that the main house with its wings contained something like thirty rooms, Wake Bannister only used three of them: his office, his bedroom, and a small dining room off the kitchen. For the most part the rest of the house was clean and well-kept— and empty, except when there were guests.

A light was on in the office, and Britt entered without knocking. Hugo Meeker was talking to Wake, and he made the polite gesture of getting up to leave when Wake waved him back. It was all right with Britt, too. Ever since he could remember, there had been no secrets from Hugo, and sometimes in the past Hugo had gentled Bannister's harsh discipline to his son. Britt liked him.

"Stick around, Hugo," Britt said and sat down.

"Who's the company?" Bannister asked dryly, coming abruptly to the point. It had been a long time since Britt had tried to lie to his father. He didn't now, knowing it was useless.

"Some saddle bum Buck Tolleston wants to hold for that Wagon Mound bank hold-up."

Bannister frowned a little. "You mean you took him away from Buck?"

"Not exactly. He was listenin' in on a conversation I didn't want repeated."

"With whom?" Wake asked gently.

"Martha Tolleston."

Hugo Meeker almost smiled. He liked young Britt because he had a lot of his old man's characteristi̶ ̶and he was the only person—with the single exception̶ ̶Hugo himself—who was not afraid to stand up to the o̶ ̶man. He watched Wake now.

"I heard about that," Wake said. "I wondered if ̶ ̶tell me."

"Why shouldn't I?"

Wake said idly, "You don't take this feud betwe̶ ̶Buck and me very serious, do you, son?"

"Not a heap," Britt admitted, smiling a little. "Besides, it's your fight, not mine."

Wake looked over at Hugo. "I'm close to sixty," he said. "Your uncle Ted is a pretty sick man and he's fifty-five. All your kin around here are rattle-brained. When I die, you'll inherit this feud."

"No, thanks."

"It's not a question of wantin' to," Wake insisted. "If you don't fight, you'll go down."

"When Buck's gone, the feud'll die, anyway," Britt said.

"The—uh—little lady wants it that way, too?" Wake asked mildly.

"That's about it."

Wake said sharply, "You want to marry her, Britt?"

"Yes."

Wake nodded, looking over at Hugo, whose face was expressionless behind his cigarette.

Wake pulled out a cigar case and lighted a smoke and
then leaned back in his chair. At first he paid no attention to Britt, and Britt waited, knowing there was something to come.

Finally Wake said, "Ever hear why Tolleston and I
hate each other the way we do, Britt?"

"I never heard you say it."

"You've likely heard we were just two men that one
country couldn't hold, is all. Both bull-headed, both
ambitious, both want to be leaders, both like power.
That's about what you've heard, isn't it?"

"About."

Wake nodded. "There's some truth in that. If we
didn't have any other reason, we might use that one. It's
logical." His gaze rested now on Britt. "But it's something more than that, son. Maybe it's time you heard it."

Hugo cleared his throat. "It is, Wake."

"I'll begin with Buck Tolleston and me settlin' down
in the Big Bend country after the war, because that's
where I first knew him. Cattle business wasn't much
then—and it was hard. A man needed a wife. I got one—
your mother, Britt. You've seen pictures of her. Sweetest
face I ever saw. Buck Tolleston wanted her, too, but I
won. That was all right, or at least it would have been
to a decent man. But not to Buck Tolleston. I was strug-
glin' to get a foothold in that country then, and I was
growin'. But Tolleston was bigger and besides that, he
had a bunch of his kinfolks settled around him. The
night before I married your mother, she and I talked it
over. It was pretty plain that Buck Tolleston and me
could never be friends, and if we couldn't be friends, we
was bound to be enemies. I asked Amy what she thought
we ought to do—stick there and fight the Tollestons or
move on to new range. She said stick. Well, we did.

"We stuck until I got hold of a good spread. I went
over my head to get it, way over. I hadn't even got a

crop of calves from my herd when it happened." Wake continued more quietly: "I was framed for a murder of a nester."

"By Buck," Hugo put in.

"Your mother was carryin' you then, Britt, but that didn't seem to make no difference. I went to prison—for six years."

"And served every day of it," Hugo said harshly, watching Britt.

Wake went on. "The spread was lost, of course. Three weeks before you was born, your mother was turned out—by one of the Tollestons. Folks down there were pretty scarce then, Britt, and none of them was our friends. I'll just skip what happened after that—five and a half years of it—and tell you what your mother did. She cooked down in a Mexican's place on the border until I come out of jail. When I went to jail, she was a woman in all her beauty. When I come out, she was an old woman—ugly, work-worn, consumptive, and wretched. Down there is where Hugo found her."

Hugo cleared his throat. "She used to tie you under the big table there in the kitchen and give you a red chili to play with. She did that because it wasn't safe for a gringo kid to play in the plaza then. Those Mexicans would ride 'em down."

"Hugo was with her when I found her," Wake went on, his voice emotionless, almost flat. "She died right after that—thanks to Buck Tolleston."

Britt's face was grave, a little pale, and he was leaning forward in his chair.

"After that, I turned outlaw," Wake said. "Not many people here know that. I wrote to my brother Will in Tennessee to come down and bring all the Bannister kin that would come. He did. He brought five boys with him. In a year, we'd killed half a dozen Tolleston hands or kin, fired Buck Tolleston's spread three times, stole a

good half his herds, and we was doin' well for ourselves.
Buck Tolleston knew who was doin' it, and he couldn't
fight us. So he picked up and moved to here. I followed
him. And I reckon you know the rest of it."

"Or can guess it," Hugo put in quietly. "Buck ain't
d yet. He will be."

Wake Bannister said no more. He lighted his cigar,
hich had gone out, and then waited for Britt to say
omething. Britt looked at the Stetson held between his
knees. Finally he stood up and looked down at his father.

"I—I never knew this, dad. I—why didn't you tell me?"
he asked huskily.

"A young man has to get a lot of things out of his sys-
tem, Britt, before he's worth much. I was givin' you time
to do just that. But I reckon the time's up."

"I reckon it is," Britt said gently.

"I knew you were seein' this Tolleston girl. I thought
it was some of your hellery, or just plain contrariness,
because you thought I wouldn't like it. Now, I reckon
you're ready to know the kind of blood that runs in the
Tolleston veins."

"Or don't run," Hugo said.

Britt said earnestly, "Dad, I swear I've never told her
anything about us over here that would—"

"I know that," Wake said. "It's never even entered my
mind you had, son. What's past is past. And now, either
you bear your share of squarin' things up, or you don't.
Which'll it be?"

"I'm with you; I would have been for ten years back if
I'd known this."

"There's been time enough," Hugo said. "There ain't
now. The time's here."

Britt looked swiftly at his father, his face strained.
"You mean you're goin' to kill Tolleston?"

Buck smiled faintly. "Nothin' of that kind, Britt. If
I'd wanted to kill him, I could have done it years ago.

No, I'm goin' to ruin him first, clean him out of everything he owns, and the rest of his bunch with him. Wardecker and his Forked Lightning, Lou Hasker and his Chain Link, Wurdemann and his Running W, Miles Kindry and his Rocking K, Wes Anders and his Seven A, Blindloss, Sweetser, Winterhoven, and Frank Pillsbury—all of them will go down with him. And when I have them licked, when Buck Tolleston looks around him and sees he's got nothin'—not even a horse to ride out of the country with—then I'll be satisfied. I may kill him then, but if I do, it will only be a kindness to hi^ ."

Britt said quietly, "How?"

"Sit down, son. We don't start tonight."

Face grim, Britt sat down. Some of his youth an^ arrogant coltishness had fallen away from him in th^ few minutes, and it was as if he had finally and irrevo^ ably passed into man's estate. He sat down and rolled a smoke with unsteady fingers.

"I don't think you knew it," Bannister began, "but I've had one of Buck Tolleston's hands in my pay. He brings me word that Buck suspects we hired these five Montana hardcases to rob his bank—along with McWilliams and this prisoner he was bringin' back. Well, Buck was right."

"You mean those men out in the old bunk house are the robbers?" Britt asked slowly.

"That's it. I paid them."

Britt appeared to reserve his decision, for he said nothing.

Bannister went on: "Buck will receive word that his hunch was right. We were behind the hold-up. All right, he aims to use this knowledge to band all the San Patricio ranchers together for a raid on Bull Foot. He will, too, because that bank robbery touched them where it hurts the most—in their pocketbooks. They'll meet some night soon and ride out of San Patricio down here."

"Then what?" Britt asked curiously.

"We'll let them burn Bull Foot—or rather we'll warn the merchants and let them fight. But we—all the Bannisters and all the Bannister kin and all the hands they employ—will be over in San Patricio. With luck, we ought to burn Wagon Mound out, and every big ranch that stands over in that country."

"Then what?" Britt repeated.

Wake Bannister smiled. It seemed that his son had a head on him, after all.

"That," Bannister said, "will remain a secret, Britt. Not because I don't trust you, not even because I wouldn't ask your advice—because I'm going to, soon— but because I'm not sure, myself. You'll know when I do, just as Hugo will."

Britt stared into his hat a full moment, taking in all that he had heard. It was a large dose for one night, and he wanted to get away by himself.

He said, "Is that all, dad?"

When Bannister said, "Yes," Britt got up and walked to the door. Midway, he paused. "About this man I brought home. What about him?"

"Yes, what about him?"

"I—he overheard Martha Tolleston and me talkin'. Buck sent him. Rather than let him go back and tell Buck about it, I brought him over."

"Who is he?"

"McWilliams's prisoner. You remember. He's wanted for that Mimbres canyon robbery last year." He hesitated. "You see, dad, I told Martha I wouldn't turn him over to the law here."

Bannister said, "You gave her your word; keep it. Besides, the boy's not guilty. That's one of Sheriff Monkhouse's tricks to cover up his blunders, just as most of his actions are."

"What'll I do with him?"

"Turn him loose."

Britt colored a little. "I can't do that. I reckon he'd ride back to Buck and tell him."

"And if he did?"

"I promised her," Britt said simply. "I reckon I can keep my word."

"Yes. Keep him, then."

Britt went out. Outside, under the stars, the world seemed to have changed a little. He did not know how, exactly, but he knew why. The stars were less bright, the air less keen, and he felt a new kind of weariness, one that was not physical, but which seemed to crawl through him like a fever.

CHAPTER NINE

MITCH BUDROW GOT IN close to daylight. He remembered what Buck had told him about bringing back the word to him immediately, so after he had stripped the saddle from his horse and turned him into the corral, he passed the bunk house and headed for the house.

At Buck's office door he knocked loudly. It was a full minute before a light appeared and Buck opened the door. His hair was rumpled and he was in his underwear and Levis.

"You," he said, surprise in his voice. "Come in."

Putting the lamp on the desk, he indicated a chair. "Sit down."

"Maybe I shouldn't have woke you—"

"What'd you find?" Buck demanded.

"I drifted in yesterday and hung around the hotel most of the mornin' hittin' ranchers for jobs. I only picked the ones I heard was full-handed. When they got used to me bein' there, I drifted over to the saloon—the Melodian. Hugo Meeker was there, and—"

"How'd you know him?" Buck cut in.

"Asked the bartender. Besides, he was ridin' a horse with a Dollar brand. That's what made me ask."

"Go on."

"He's foreman for Bannister, the barkeep said. Well, he was buckin' the tiger—"

"It don't sound like him."

"That's what the barkeep said. That's how I found out it was Meeker. When this gent come in and started for the faro table, the barkeep's jaw fell open, and that is—"

"Go on," Buck said impatiently.

Mitch, sweating, drew a deep breath and continued. "I'd been sort of mouthy up till then. After that, I shut up and watched. It wasn't long before one of these Montana hardcases drifted in. I saw Meeker look up at him and then slide his look away. Dead face, never a sign he knowed him. This rider drifts into a back room. I watched the door. Pretty soon, another one of these Montana boys drifted in from the dance hall. He went in the same room. Hugo quit playin' faro and watched a poker game a while. Then he drifted back and went in the same room."

"The one the Montana men went in?"

"That's right."

"Then what?"

"I hung around for another two hours. They called for drinks three times."

"That don't sound like Hugo."

"I know it. That's what—"

"—the bartender said," Buck finished impatiently. "Get on."

"About sundown, this Meeker come out, got his horse, and rode off. Ten minutes later, the two hardcases drifted out. They must have killed the bottle because they looked like a cat that'd just ate the fish. One of them took the faro table and cleaned up five hundred and lost it on one card. He turned away and laughed and said, 'Hell, I'll bust that before I quit.' Then they sat down to a table of poker, and that's where I left 'em."

"Out in the open," Buck murmured.

"I thought you'd want to know," Mitch said innocently.

Buck only looked at him.

"Is it all right?" Mitch asked.

"All right?" Buck echoed. He smiled slightly, and it was more of a grimace than a smile. "Are you sure about all this, Budrow? Plumb sure?"

"It happened that way," Mitch said. "Maybe if I'd waited I'd of got their names. I thought you'd want to know about—"

Buck grunted, silencing Mitch. He looked fondly at him. "You couldn't have done better, son, if you'd brought their names."

Mitch made a diffident gesture. "It was luck, mostly."

"Go get some sleep," Buck said. "I've got all the proof I need."

Mitch went out to the bunk house. There was a chorus of snores which Mitch did not seem to hear. Once in his blankets, he got to thinking about Buck Tolleston. A salty little devil, a good boss, in his way. And then Mitch tried not to remember that. When someone's got a gun to your ear, you aren't much interested in anything else, he reflected, not even people who are good to you. Before he dropped off to sleep, he heard Buck walking toward the corral.

Buck didn't even wait for breakfast. Now that he had definite proof of his suspicions, there were other considerations more important than filling his belly. He rode into Wagon Mound in mid-morning, tied his horse in front of the sheriff's office, and went inside.

Wardecker was not there, but Wally was. Buck ignored him and would not condescend to tell him his business. Out on the step, Buck paused. There was work for him at the bank, tallying losses, liquidating the investments of the people who had to have money and have it quickly. Patton was dead, and Buck was bewildered by the task that faced him. He eyed the bank with distaste. Just then he spotted Will Wardecker coming up the sidewalk alone, his old body hunched comfortably over the crutch.

Buck turned and said over his shoulder to Wally, "Here comes Will. I want to talk to him alone."

Wally obligingly stepped out. Wardecker greeted Buck and went inside, and Buck shut the door after him and followed him to his creaky swivel chair.

"Well, you think I'm a pretty hard man, don't you? Plumb suspicious, unreasonable, quick-tempered, and a little wild in the way my thinkin' runs," Buck said mildly.

Wardecker looked at him shrewdly. "I'm wrong about somethin'. What is it this time?"

"First thing is, your prisoner, Webb Cousins, jumped the country. Rode down into Wintering County with another hombre—likely a man sent up from there to get him. I put Cousins on a windbroke horse to—well, never mind. Anyway, he joined this other rider and they rode over into Wintering, we think."

"Who said so?"

"My men. They tracked 'em as far as the county line. Mac made camp there last night, waitin' for daylight, and sent word back to me. They're headin' for Wintering."

Wardecker said, "What've you been doin' to the boy, Buck?"

"Doin'!" Tolleston flared up. "Feedin' him, givin' him a decent bed, decent work, as much freedom as I could!"

"Then it don't seem logical he could have run for Wintering, when they want him over there."

Buck smiled thinly. This was what he had been waiting for. "Not unless they was bringin' him home to pay him for a good job of bank robbin' done."

"I don't believe it," Wardecker said gently.

"No? All right, listen to this." He told him about Mitch Budrow's visit to Bull Foot, and what he had seen. Wardecker listened intently, polishing the bowl of his cold pipe with his hand.

"Of course," Buck finished sarcastically, "those hardcases just struck up an acquaintance with Meeker. Maybe they wanted a job, bein' broke. Maybe this Cousins decided to run down and give hisself up, preferring jail to what I was givin' him. Maybe it's just coincidence and what the hell do we care—they never hurt us."

Wardecker grimaced. "Easy, Buck."

Tolleston said nothing. His triumph was complete, so he waited.

"You can trust this Mitch Budrow?" Wardecker asked.

"You know him. What do you think?"

"I allus liked him. Besides, he owes you somethin'. I'd say, yes."

"All right."

Buck waited. Wardecker packed his pipe and lighted it and sat there, arms folded across the back of his neck, staring at the blue smoke he was exhaling.

"Hell," he said quietly. He looked up at Tolleston. "What's next, Buck?"

"Cattlemen's meeting."

"And?"

"If they've got any fight, it'll be out of my hands. If they ain't, then I reckon I'll have to do somethin' I've been keeping away from most of my life."

"Kill Wake Bannister?"

"That's right."

"When'll this meetin' be?"

"I left a note to Mac to send Mitch Budrow into town this afternoon. I want them all to hear it from him. The board of directors of the bank is meetin' this afternoon. That includes almost every cattleman we'll want. Those that ain't there and don't live far we can send for now. And those that live too far will be into town anyway, I reckon, to hear what the bank decides to do, and if it will close down. That bank meetin' can wait until this is finished."

Tolleston was right. Almost every cattleman of any

size, for one reason or another, was in town by noon. Those who were directors, Buck requested to gather for the meeting in the bank. The others were asked to attend, since Buck had made plain that it was to be an open meeting, mainly to ask advice. No one in town, outside of Buck and Wardecker and Mitch Budrow, who had arrived at noon, knew the real purpose of the meeting.

It was held in the bank, and as soon as Buck had recognized the faces of all the men he needed, he directed Mitch to lock the door. It was a grim gathering. All of these men were ranchers, all either stockholders in the bank, or men whose notes the bank held. Directly or indirectly, its welfare was a force in their lives, and this was reflected in their faces. Some of them had been in the posse which had pursued the robbers. That day they had been deeper into Wintering County than ever before and they had not turned back because of fear. It takes time to track fugitives, and these men knew from bitter experience that the deeper they went into Wintering territory and the more time it took, the graver the chance was of being ambushed. Only when the men sent ahead to scout returned to report that a small posse of Wintering men, getting bigger as it came, was approaching, did they turn back. And in that moment many of them realized with bitterness exactly what they had been brewing for themselves for fifteen years. Some wanted to return, band together, and come back and clean up Wintering County, paving the way to the capture of the bank robbers. Others suggested mediation, a parley, a plea for help. Still others were ready to quit, sure that neither of the other plans would succeed. But whatever they believed, they knew that this was the darkest time in their lives. Yesterday Buck Tolleston had purposely avoided talking to them, inciting them. He could win a few over to the side of violence, but not enough. Today he thought he could.

He rapped on Patton's desk with his gun butt. His

listeners were scattered on the counter, the other two desks, the chairs against the wall.

He began temperately: "I told you men this was to be a meetin' of the men interested in the bank, for the purpose of seein' what could be done." He paused. "I know what can be done. It don't concern the bank. It concerns all of us. But before I go on, I want your oaths that what's said in this room—every last detail of it—will be kept quiet. Any man that don't feel like givin' his word can step out." When none moved, he said, "Then I take it that your oaths have been given. Is that right?"

They nodded or said "yes," or merely looked at each other, wondering what was coming.

"The news I have to give," Buck went on, his manner increasingly aggressive and terrierlike, "is damn simple! It's this. I have proof that men over in Wintering County backed the hold-up of our bank and that they are giving the bank robbers refuge there now."

Buck saw a half dozen men rise out of their chairs, but he wasn't watching them. They were the hotheads, like himself. He was watching three of the older ranchers— Lee Wurdemann, a man who sided him in the old days and now owned the second biggest spread in the county; Wes Anders, big, gentle, peaceful; Miles Kindry, mild as May and hog fat—and one of the younger ones, Lou Hasker. It was at Hasker that Buck looked longest, because Hasker's Chain Link was the county's biggest ranch, employing the most men, and because Lou Hasker, above all people, had irritated Buck the most in the past with his indifference. Hasker was young, able son of an able father, red-haired, drawling, and quiet. The bank held his note for forty thousand dollars. Thirty thousand of it, earned by a daring drive through the Silver Horn Breaks a month ago with more cattle than had left San Patricio County in ten years, was deposited in the bank, awaiting the month when half the sum fell due. As things stood now, Hasker was ruined, and Buck knew it. The only change in Hasker's face now was a little tightening of his jaw muscles. His cool voice cut through the hum of swelling talk.

"Can you prove that, Buck?"

Buck gestured to Mitch Budrow. "Here's the man I sent down to Bull Foot. He's new to them people, so I reckoned he could get away with it. He'll tell you. I only want to add that I have trusted him in the past and found him reliable." He turned to Mitch. "Tell them what you told me."

Mitch, showing a quiet confidence he did not feel, told in a level, matter-of-fact voice substantially what he had told Tolleston. The assembly heard him out in utter silence, and when he was finished, they still did not speak.

Suddenly, Lew Hasker said, "Budrow, are you sure you know Hugo Meeker?"

"No, I ain't," Mitch said. "I took the bartender's word, that and the brand on his horse. But I can tell you what the man I saw looks like."

"Go ahead."

Mitch pretended to recollect a moment. Some warning voice inside him told him that this was his last chance to do the right thing, and that by the time he had finished this description he would have taken the choice between being damned or dead. He wanted to live.

"This gent, I should say, come from Texas. I wouldn't say how old he is, because he likely looked the way he does now when he was twenty and he'll look that way when he's sixty. My guess would be forty-five, though. He's got washed-out hair, and eyes between a light gray and a blue and they're shallow. He's got a hatchet face, long, thin mouth; he's lean and his cheeks is sunk and he smokes without taking the cigarette from his mouth. He's close to six feet, might weigh a hundred and sixty, and he moves slow. He don't smile neither."

"What kind of horse does he ride?"

"A blue roan branded Dollar on the left hip."

A murmur of assent rose from some of the men.

Hasker went on doggedly. "That's Hugo. What about these hardcases?"

Mitch went on stubbornly: "The man I noticed first was about forty. He was wearin' a flat-brimmed Stetson dented four ways. He had deep-set light eyes and the skin was pulled tight acrost his cheeks. He was thin and not very tall, and I noticed he was chewin' on a match the whole time I watched him."

Wally half rose out of his seat. "That's the man that covered me on the steps, Hasker."

"The other one—" Mitch began, but Hasker waved him quiet. For a long time, Hasker said nothing. He had a coin in his hand which he examined thoughtfully. Because he had been the first to question Mitch, men were waiting for him to act. He looked up at Buck and pocketed the coin.

"That's good enough for me, Buck. I'll back your play."

The whole roomful, as of one accord, seconded him.

Buck swiftly addressed the older men. "How about you, Wurdemann, Anders, Kindry? And you, Sweetser and Pillsbury? And you, Dale? Do you think the way Hasker does?"

They said "yes," and said it emphatically.

"Then," Buck said, "I step down. You're willin' to fight for what's been taken from you. So am I. I'll let you decide how."

"Stay there, Buck," Hasker said. "You've been tryin' to rawhide us into this for years. You were right, I reckon. If we'd taken a fightin' hand in this sooner, we'd never be where we are today. Many's the time you hoped you could do this. How do you plan it?"

Buck answered swiftly, "Ride into Bull Foot, burn it

down. Burn the courthouse, all the records, all the stores, all the loadin' pens. And I'll tell you why. Because the whole town—lock, stock, and barrel—is owned by the Bannisters. You can hurt more Bannisters that way than ridin' all over the county—all except one, that is. That's Wake. When you've burned the town, then put the Dollar spread in ashes and you've got Wintering licked."

"They've got a railroad," somebody objected. "It's easy to build up again."

"Burn it down again," Buck said. "Rustle their stuff, poison their water holes, fire their spreads. It'll take more than one raid, but the point is—keep hammerin'!"

"They'll strike back," someone else said.

"Of course they will!" Buck said angrily. "Hell, it's war, ain't it? All we want is warnin' and a chance to strike the first blow." He quieted down. "That's my plan. If you can think of a better one, let's hear it."

No one could. The Bannisters, all of the same family, had a hold on Wintering County that was almost ownership. Put them down and you put Wintering down. First, the many Bannisters, then the biggest one. Wake Bannister might receive news of the town's being plundered, but he would not lift a finger to avenge it. But if the forces were directed against Wake Bannister's Dollar outfit first, he could, and would, summon the whole county to fight for him. Better to make sure of the town before tackling Wake, so the ranchers reasoned. And it was out of the question to split forces; if that were done, both attacks might fail.

When the plan was agreed upon, Buck looked at Wardecker, who leaned against the back wall smoking his pipe, taking no part in this. Buck only grinned at him and then turned to Hasker.

"I don't have to tell you this has got to be kept secret, Lou. That's why the doors are locked and I made you give your word."

Hasker agreed. One slip and their chances of revenge were destroyed. But, as Hasker looked around the room, he could not pick out a single man who had not suffered a loss at the hands of Wintering County. They would be unlikely to betray the secret.

"We'll have to go careful," Hasker said quietly. He turned to the lone storekeeper in the room. "Bob, how many shells have you got in stock?"

"Cases of forty-fives and thirty-thirties."

"Then we'll draw on you, and it'll have to be done secretly, too."

They discussed this, and many other things, such as the best trail to take to Bull Foot, the best time, the number of men wanted, who the leaders would be, what the plan of attack would be once in Bull Foot, how the big bunch would be split up.

Mitch Budrow, toying idly with his hat, stood by Wardecker and did not miss a word. He contrived to give the appearance of an ordinary cow-puncher in a gathering of his superiors, who does not expect to be asked for advice and who would be stricken dumb if he was.

Wardecker pitied him, the unconscious instrument of so much death and destruction. He wondered if Mitch Budrow in after years would not look back on this day with disgust and remember it as a mistake that could not be written off.

CHAPTER TEN

WEBB SPENT HIS FIRST NIGHT in the single bunk at the far corner of the bunk house chained by leg irons to the upright. He spent the first day chained to the leg of the heavy table on which he and Lute and Shorty and another wry-faced Northerner played poker. No one from the main house came near him, and the day was dull for them all. Lute wanted to ride that afternoon, but he was afraid to take Webb with him. By night the Montana men regretted their bargain, and, like children who have been kept in a house all day by rain, were in a savage mood by bedtime.

The next morning, Lute greeted Webb in a better humor.

"I'm goin' to take these things off you today."

"You might chain me to an anvil," Webb said dryly.

"I might. But I think I'm a good enough shot that I don't have to."

Webb knew this was a warning, but he was glad of this new freedom. If he made just one bad move, he knew Lute would kill him, and do it cheerfully. Lute was tough, wise, seasoned, experienced enough in things of this sort that he was far more effective in keeping Webb a prisoner than a strong jail would have been.

At breakfast over in the bunk house that morning, Webb found that Lute would talk. It seemed that Lute and his men were allowed the freedom of the ranch—all except the big house. They could ride wherever they chose, except north and into Bull Foot. They could drink all they wanted, and had an account at the store and the *cantina*. But they were forbidden to associate with the ranch hands and to talk to strangers. That seemed liberal enough to Webb, opening many avenues of possible escape.

Back at the bunk house, Britt Bannister was waiting for him, his face a little grim, so that Webb wondered if, after all, Bannister was going to turn him over to the law.

Outside, he and Britt Bannister squatted against the wall and rolled smokes, while Lute watched them idly from the door.

"I'm sorry I had to do this," Bannister began.

"I'll bet you are."

"The reason I'm sorry," Bannister went on, "is because I don't want to do it. Nothing would please me more than having you ride over to Buck Tolleston and tell him what you heard."

Webb looked sharply at him, then away. "Sure," he mocked. "Why don't you, then?"

"Because I gave that killer's wench my word," Britt said bitterly.

Webb simply pivoted on his heel, unfolding like a coiled spring and drove his fist into Britt Bannister's face. Bannister's head snapped back against the wall and then he slumped over on his side and lay still. Webb looked up to see Lute's gun trained on him.

Lute walked over to him. "Now, why did you do that?"

"Ask him," Webb said thickly, and started for the bunk house.

Lute bawled for his partner, who took over the job of carting Britt away while Lute watched Webb. Webb stood there in the door of the bunk house, rubbing his stinging knuckles. He didn't know why he had done that. The action was purely automatic, a thing he would have done had he heard any decent woman slandered. But he wondered what had got into Britt, what change had come over him since last night.

In a few minutes Britt walked over to the door, declining the help Lute's partner offered. He paused in front of Webb, his hand to his jaw.

"Maybe you don't know where you are," he said thickly.

"About two steps from a shot in the back."

Britt said jeeringly, "So she looks good to you, eh?"

"Good enough to keep her name out of your mouth."

Lute put in quietly to Webb: "Son, you spraddle him again, and I'm liable to get mad."

Britt ignored Lute, as did Webb. They stood perhaps six feet apart, sizing each other up, glaring at each other like two wary dogs who only need a word to make them join battle.

Then Britt sneered. "She's killer's spawn, Cousins. You can like her if you want, but you can't change that. Her old man's a murderer and all her kin are as bad. She is, too." It was not the anger in Britt's face that Webb noted; it was the bitterness in his voice.

"That's a different story from what I overheard yesterday," Webb said.

"Shut up damn you!"

Webb went on: "It seemed yesterday you both agreed to use your heads in this ruckus when nobody else was doin' it. You both hated this feud." He smiled quietly. "What's the matter? Have a bad dream?"

With a snarl in his throat, Britt came at him. Webb put both hands on the door-sill, raised his foot, and stopped Britt's rush by placing a boot in his chest and pushing. Bannister went down, sprawling on his back. Webb turned to Lute: "What am I goin' to do, let him beat me up?"

"If you're smart, you will," Lute said.

"Then I'm not."

He stepped off the door-sill to the ground, facing Britt, who was just rising. Bannister did not wait a second. He lunged at Webb, arms flailing. Webb chopped down on Britt's forearm, grunting as the deflected blow caught him in the stomach. His left hand, ready cocked, looped over in a hook that caught young Bannister behind the ear. It was as if sudden paralysis took hold of him. His guard dropped and he stood there shaking his head groggily.

Suddenly Hugo Meeker's voice whipped out across the bright morning. "Hit him again and I'll kick you from here to Bull Foot."

Webb looked up. Hugo was lounging against a corner of the bunk house, a cigarette pasted to his lower lip. Webb let his hands down to his side and stepped away.

"I've licked him twice in fifteen minutes. If you don't want him mussed up, take him away."

Hugo slouched over. He grabbed Britt by the shirt and tilted his head back and then slapped him sharply a half dozen times. Then he said to Lute's partner, "Take him over to the main bunk house."

Britt gone, Hugo turned to Webb. He had not yet taken the cigarette from his mouth. "Because that kid can't scrap, don't think the rest of us can't."

"I hadn't even thought about it," Webb said. "But when somebody swarms all over me, I swarm back."

Hugo looked at him coldly and did not even wait for him to finish, but walked away. Webb sat down on the door-sill, breathing hard. Lute came out and squatted against the wall and rolled a smoke.

"Now you've done it," he said impersonally.

"Sure."

They were quiet a long time. Webb built his morning smoke and dragged its raw bite into his lungs. Lute, by his own predatory reasoning, had pretty well called the turn.

Webb cursed himself. He was in enough of a jam without leaping to the defense of a girl he had seen only twice in his life, and who was the daughter of a man who was persecuting him. If he had expected any favors here, he might as well forget it.

"Who was that man that took him off?"

"Hugo Meeker, the ramrod."

Webb smoked moodily. Presently Lute said, "What're you here for, son?"

Webb told him the whole story from the time they had met in Wagon Mound. When he was finished, Lute said, "But this train stick-up? Was you in on it or was this a frame-up?"

Webb, who had told his story idly and without much interest, suddenly came to attention, aware of the implications of Lute's question. If he told Lute he was guilty, wasn't there a possibility that Lute might look upon him as one of the fraternity to which he belonged? He hesitated.

"Okay," Lute said idly. "None of my business."

Webb smiled. "Hell, yes, I was guilty. Do you think I'd 'a' let them bring me clean over here if I could've helped it."

"I was wonderin'," Lute said, looking at him.

At this moment, Shorty, who had taken Britt to the bunk house, returned. He sat down beside Lute and glanced over at Webb.

"If I wasn't bein' paid to hold you here, I'd tell you to take a horse and high-tail it," he told Webb.

Webb spat carelessly.

Then Shorty's attention was shifted. He said to Lute, "Somethin's up around here."

"Like what?"

"Ain't a rider goin' out this mornin'. They're all around the bunk house, waitin' for orders."

"Talk to any of 'em?"

"Not me," Shorty said. "I'm gettin' paid to be a little choosy about who I talk with."

Lute laughed and they talked of other things. But Webb wondered. Bannister must be expecting trouble of some sort—or planning it. When there was a break in the conversation, he asked idly, "How many hands has Bannister got here?"

"There's about thirty over there now," Shorty said.

"Doin' what?" Lute wanted to know.

"The last I seen a good half of 'em was leadin' their ponies over to get shod."

Webb scowled. He was about to suggest having a look when Lute said, "I could stand a drink."

"Let's go," Shorty said.

They all went into the *cantina* together. It was a shabby adobe, its shelves lined with cheap wines and whiskies and *tequilas*.

Webb had a drink with Lute and Shorty, and then they moved on up to Mooney's store, where they sat on the broad porch and watched the activity.

The plaza on which the store fronted had a holiday air about it. Riders conversed in several groups and waited while the anvil over in Symonds's blacksmith shop clanged steadily. Webb noticed that the Dollar hands apparently had two duties: to take their horses over to be shod and to drop into Mooney's for shells.

Lute watched it all with mounting curiosity.

"Looks like a fight," he said once.

"Find out," Webb suggested.

Lute grunted. But he was only human. After a half hour on Mooney's porch, Lute lounged to his feet, saying to Shorty, "When you see me come out of the *cantina*, come around in back of this place," and he headed across the plaza.

In a few minutes, he came out of the *cantina*, and

Shorty said to Webb, "Walk around in back."

Lute, when he joined them, had a bottle of *tequila* hidden in his shirt front. He grinned sheepishly at Webb. "I'm goin' to find out what this is all about."

They ended up at the main horse corral, which was in charge of a Mexican wrangler. The three of them lined up on the top rail and waited for the wrangler to come over to them. He did, eventually, and Lute yarned with him about horses. Already the wrangler had an excellent opinion of these five Montana men who rode such good horses, and he listened to Lute's sage observations with the air of a pupil listening to a master. Lute, still talking, pulled out his bottle of *tequila*, offered Shorty and Webb a drink, which they accepted, and then offered the bottle to the Mexican. He looked around uncomfortably and then said, "Come with me, señor. Mc, I'm not s'p_e to dreenk."

Lute laughed and went with him into the barn. They were gone a long time. When Lute finally returned without the bottle, he motioned the others off the fence and when they were safely away, said, "I got it."

"What is it?" Shorty asked.

"He didn't know for sure. But he thinks there's a raid bein' planned."

"Hell, I could 'a' guessed that. Where?"

"San Patricio County so the talk goes."

Webb listened with expressionless face, but he was thinking of what had been told him that night in Tolleston's house.

Then Budrow had somehow learned that these hard-cases were working for Bannister, and he had taken the news back to Tolleston. Which meant, if Tolleston's hunch was correct, that the San Patricio ranchers had already banded together for a raid. Was this arming on the part of Bannister a defensive measure?

That afternoon Webb was to find out, for Hugo

Meeker came into the bunk house. At his entrance the lackadaisical poker game was suspended.

Hugo, cigarette in lower lips, came to the point immediately. "Noticed all the commotion outside?"

"Uh-huh," Lute told him.

"It's here," Hugo said. "Tonight the San Patricio outfit aims to raid Bull Foot, and then the spread here. They don't know we know it. About the time they get deep into Winterin', three quarters of their spreads over there will be burnin'. So will Wagon Mound."

Lute whistled. "Anything for us to do?" he asked.

"No. If this thing works out, those raiders from across the line will run into a surprise in Bull Foot. They'll be lucky if a fifth of them get out alive. But they aim to raid this spread, too. Now I don't reckon they'll still have that same idea when they leave Bull Foot, but just in case they do, we want to be ready for 'em."

He went on to explain that the bulk of the Dollar riders would be over in San Patricio, with only a skeleton crew here at the ranch and in town. The Mexicans had been armed, so that they could defend the place. Meeker wanted Lute and his men to draw ammunition from Mooney and be ready to assist in the defense if they should be needed. The triangle over at the blacksmith shop would sound the warning in case of raid. There was hardly any possibility of one, Meeker reiterated, but they wanted to make sure.

After he was gone, the play was resumed. Webb stared at his cards, but he was not seeing them. This then, would spell the finish of San Patricio's revolt. Its men would walk into a trap, its homes and ranches and town would be burned. The thought of it made Webb a little sick. He thought of gentle, reasonable Wardecker and what would happen to him. And to Tolleston, not gentle, not reasonable, but, Webb believed, a man who might have a kinder side. And to Martha Tolleston, who had put her trust and hope in a man who thought her a "killer's wench," a man who knew that by night she would be homeless and fatherless and who would help to make her so.

"Wake up, cowboy. It's checked to you," Lute's voice was saying. Webb grinned a little and resumed playing. But he was thinking, and the more he thought, the more absent-minded he became.

Finally Lute, in exasperation, said, "Fella, if you played this way all the time, I'd make some money."

Webb yawned, and said carelessly, "Sure, and when you want some more, you'll hire out to a big wind like Bannister and let him kick you around for a month when you could be makin' money, big money."

Lute looked hard at him. "Leastways, I never got pulled in by a tank-town sheriff on a job yet."

"What good does it do you?" Webb drawled. "You stuck up a bank the other day. Three days later you're broke."

"And what if I am?" Lute said softly.

Webb shrugged. "Oh, nothin'. You'll sit around here like a squaw over a bucket of tea and let other riders make the money."

"Like who?" Lute said belligerently.

Webb thought a moment, then suddenly grinned and reached for the cards. "Nothin'. Forget it. I'm just sore, I reckon."

"What about?"

Webb jerked his thumb in the direction of the big house. "All those thirty-dollar-a-month cowpokes goin' on that ride and not knowin' what to do with it."

Shorty looked at Lute. "How you mean?" he said to Webb.

"Why, there's big spreads in that county. Money, horses, guns, gold."

Lute said, "Well, what about it?"

Webb shrugged and started to shuffle the deck. "Noth-in'. Only we sit here like a bunch of women, protectin' the spread of a big stuffed Stetson just because we was told to."

"We?" Lute said dryly. "You couldn't leave if you wanted to."

"That's right," Webb agreed idly. "It's a damn shame, too, because I reckon I know that county."

The seed had been planted. Webb watched it work. The game soon broke up, and they drifted out to the plaza again to watch preparations. Lute was restless, as was Shorty. The other three Montana men—Wes, Manny, and a vicious-looking one named Perry Warren—usually slept all day, drinking a little, but today they seemed to catch a little of the unrest. They, too, lounged around the plaza.

Lute started drinking in the early afternoon, and by dark he was drunk. It was the dangerous kind of drunk, Webb knew; the man got quieter, his eyes got sharper, his brain more active, and his speech was quick and hard and cruel.

Dark had just come when the Dollar riders scattered to get their mounts. Afterward, the whole cavalcade rode through the plaza and out north, Hugo Meeker, Britt Bannister, and Wake Bannister, whom Webb had never seen until now, heading them.

The Mexicans and a few odd ranch hands lined the plaza to watch their exit. Lute watched with hard, jeer-ing eyes, Webb noticed. The Montana men went back to the bunk house, but Lute stopped in at the *cantina* to get a couple of bottles. Back in the bunk house, he did not join the perpetual poker game, but drank quietly, moodily. Webb was playing with a patience that was close to the breaking point.

But he was not surprised when Lute said suddenly, "How good do you know San Patricio, Red?"

"Fair. I know how to get to two or three ranches."

"Big ones?"

"Uh-huh."

"Which ones?"

"Tolleston's. The Chain Link."

CHAPTER ELEVEN

Lute grunted and lapsed into silence. But Shorty was watching him now, and the poker game seemed to lack interest for everybody concerned. Presently, Shorty said morosely, "I don't hear no raid alarm."

Lute shifted restlessly. Everyone in the room, including Webb, was looking to Lute for leadership.

Suddenly Shorty said, "Why don't we go, Lute?"

"And have one of these Mexes tell Meeker? Huh-uh."

"How they gonna know?" Shorty persisted.

"They can come over here and look."

Shorty was silent a moment, his forehead creased, his pig eyes greedy.

"How about just a couple of us goin'?"

Lute did not answer immediately. The other three hardcases seconded Shorty.

"All right," Lute said, rising. "Two of us'll go, and three stay here. But I'm goin', see?" He looked at them belligerently. "Anybody want to argue that?" Nobody did, and then he explained why. "Cousins has got to go because he knows the way. I got to guard him—unless I want to get a shot in the back. You boys can cut cards to see who gets to side us."

Shorty, with his accustomed luck at cards, cut a king high, and the other three, after some mild cursing, resigned themselves to staying. Lute wasted no time. He picked up a rope from the bunk, flipped up his gun, and said to Webb:

"You're goin' to ride, son. Bring the saddles, Shorty."
Shorty gave Webb his, took the others, and they went out
into the night.

Lute left Webb behind Mooney's with Shorty guard-
ing him and went to confer with the wrangler. In a few
moments he returned leading three of the big Northern
horses.

Lute made a thorough job of tying Webb's feet under
his horse's belly and tying his hands, then they mounted
and rode quietly past the corrals south, circled the spread
and once clear of the ranch buildings, headed north.

Webb figured that the Dollar riders had an hour's start
on them, but to offset this advantage they were certain
to travel slowly and carefully. They would probably head
first for Wagon Mound, and then, after it was burned,
split up into raiding parties. If Webb traveled hard and
straight, he might be able to reach Tolleston's before
Bannister's riders did. He would try.

Lute asked questions only once, and that was to find
out where they were going.

"Tolleston's Broken Arrow," Webb told him.

"Is that big?"

"Big enough."

"Any loot?"

"Plenty," Webb told him. "Do you think I'd be riding
for it like this if there wasn't?"

Webb set a stiff pace and held it and it seemed to sat-
isfy his guards. Riding through those long hours, he
turned over in his mind the chances he had of escaping.
If he could only get to the Broken Arrow before Bannister's riders, he could do something. He didn't know
how he could escape, but escape he would, and it would
have to be in time to save Tolleston's house and buildings. By the time they reached there, Lute would be
drunk. Even if he were more dangerous than usual, he

would be less careful. From Shorty, Webb had nothing to fear.

It lacked a full four hours of daylight when Webb pulled up on the lip of ridge behind the house and said, "She lies down yonder."

"No one been here yet," Lute observed with satisfaction.

He pulled the bottle from his hip pocket, had a drink with Shorty, and they dismounted.

"What's the lay down here?" Lute asked Webb.

"Untie me and I'll show you."

"You likely would," Lute observed dryly. "All the same, you stay here, fella. And I'll hobble your horse to make sure you do."

Webb chuckled. *"Bueno,* but how about leavin' me a drink for company, anyway?"

"Sure," Lute said agreeably, for the bottle was empty. Shorty hobbled Webb's horse, and before they left, Lute handed up the empty whisky bottle and laughed. Webb thanked him politely and listened to their footsteps on the rocky slope die into the silence of the night.

This was easier than he had hoped for. Waiting until he was sure they were out of hearing distance, he took the bottle in both hands and brought it down sharply on the saddle horn. It shattered, but in several large shards, two of which were in his hands. Rising up in the saddle, Webb took the half which was the top and placed the neck under him, then sat on it, wedging it between him and the swell. The razor-sharp edge stuck up and by maneuvering a little, he found that he could get his bound wrists in a position where he could drag the ropes over the glass edge. After cutting himself twice, he succeeded in sawing one strand, and then pulling, straining, manipulating it with his teeth and tugging until his wrists bled, his hands were soon free of the rope. It was the work of only a few moments to cut the rope which held his feet together and in their stirrups, and he was free.

He went quickly to the other two horses to see if either Lute or Shorty had carried a carbine in the saddle boot, but he found them both empty. Turning, he started down the slope. He was unarmed, but it would take more than the lack of a gun to stop him this night.

In the shelter of the wagon shed behind the house, he paused to get his breath and listen. Even as he was watching, he saw a light go on in the house. That would be the answer to Lute's hammering on the door. Webb broke into a run, hoping wildly that Martha Tolleston would have sense enough to answer the door with a gun. And as soon as he wished it, he thought of what Lute would do. Shoot her, probably.

At the corner of the house he slowed down and looked around it cautiously. There was Shorty standing in the light streaming from the door with a drawn gun pointing at the inside of the house. Lute, then, was already inside. The light was receding now, as if somebody had been holding a lamp and was backing into the room. Shorty stayed where he was.

Webb dropped to his knees and began to crawl forward. Shorty took a step so that he stood directly in the doorway. Webb edged closer. He could hear voices now raised in anger, and one of them was Martha Tolleston's. And then, as Webb crept forward, his hand closed over a rock. Automatically he picked it up and continued. Now he was close to the porch, and Shorty was still in the door.

Quietly, softly, he straightened up, swung a leg over the rail, had one foot directly behind Shorty, and then swung the other over.

But he didn't swing his leg high enough. His spur caught and jangled, and Shorty whipped around, swinging his Colt up.

Before Shorty had time to focus his eyes, Webb smashed the rock down on his head. Shorty sagged into Webb's arms and Webb grabbed the gun, dumped Shorty over the rail, and leaped into the doorway.

Before him, Martha Tolleston was facing Lute. Beside her stood Mrs. Partridge, the lamp in her hand.

Lute was saying, "He's got a safe, sister. Did you ever hear of a cattleman that—"

"Lute!" Webb whipped out.

Lute turned. He had holstered his gun, thinking Shorty all the protection he needed. Now he regarded Webb, and a thin smile broke over his face.

"Well, well, *compadre*. Give us a hand," he said, mildly.

"The only hand you'll get is a filled one, fella. Make your play."

Webb wanted to look at Martha, to see her face. He heard Mrs. Partridge's low moan, but he did not look at her either. It was Lute, hard-eyed, smiling narrowly, arrogantly, whom he was watching.

Lute said, "So this was a—" and he stopped, listening. The sound of someone running close to the house came to them.

Lute grinned. "All over, is it, Shorty?" he asked, looking beyond Webb.

Webb started to turn when the girl screamed. Lute, his right hand streaking for his gun, reached out with his left to yank the girl in front of him. Webb's gun shuttled up, and when hip-high, exploded deafeningly. He paused only long enough to note that Lute hunched in his chest and took a step back, dragging Martha with him, and then he whirled, to be greeted by the orange of gun blast that seemed to explode his head in a million pinwheels of stars.

When he awakened, he was lying on the ground in front of a crowd of watching horsemen. The night was bright, and he turned his head to see what made it so. There, fifty yards ahead of him, the Tolleston house was in flames. He could hear voices and raised up on an elbow. Behind him stood Martha Tolleston, her face utterly dead and expressionless. Beside her was Mrs. Partridge, crying softly, and beside her was Charley, the cook.

Mounted on a big bay beside and behind them sat Wake Bannister at the head of his riders.

Webb slowly dragged himself to his feet and started toward Martha when he stumbled and pitched on his face. It was Lute and Shorty, both dead, who had tripped him. He looked up into the cold eyes of Martha Tolleston.

Wake Bannister said, "So they didn't get you?"

Charley, the cook, looked murder at him.

"It wasn't my fault," he said grimly.

Wake Bannister chuckled and said to Webb, "You'd have deserved it, friend, if they had." And he added dryly, "Did you object to being left home tonight?"

Meeker pulled his horse over to Webb.

"I thought I told you men to guard the spread."

Webb, quietly amazed, looked over at Martha.

"Perhaps he and his friends didn't want to be left out of your picnic," she said quietly. "They were fighting over which one would make me open dad's safe."

Meeker raised his quirt and lashed it across Webb's face.

"You tinhorn," he said quietly and wheeled his horse. To one of the riders he said, "Get this man's horse and tie him on it."

Webb stood teetering there, unable at once to comprehend. And then he thought he understood. Martha Tolleston had naturally assumed that he and Shorty and Lute had come together. What Lute had said in greeting there in the house had confirmed this. What had stam-

peded the gunfight and what Lute had hoped would
turn it to his advantage was the approach of Charley,
who Lute thought was Shorty. Webb had shot Lute,
and had been tagged in turn by Charley. And Charley's
reason for running to the house was to warn Martha that
a band of riders—Bannister's raiders—was approaching.

Bannister's voice interrupted his thoughts: "Well,
boys, I guess the job is done. Let's move on." To Martha
he said, "When Buck Tolleston comes back from his
raid on Bull Foot—and I hope he doesn't—just ask him
whose idea this was, Miss Tolleston." He made a mock
bow, and gestured toward the burning house. "In this
you have the heartfelt compliments of the Bannisters.
Good night, ma'am."

A rider came up to Webb with one of the horses. Webb
mounted it dizzily. His head was sticky with blood, and
his ear numb where Charley's bullet had creased him.
The rider tied him to the saddle and Webb wearily
submitted.

His break for freedom had been futile, his attempt to
warn Martha Tolleston of the raid had turned against
him, and he was a prisoner again, and this time one who
would merit any punishment that Hugo Meeker could
think up.

Maybe he had been unwise to try it in the first place,
for she would have been unable to do anything to save
the spread. But this quiet, grave girl who held so much
courage and fire and womanliness deserved more than
this—the betrayal of the man she was to marry, and the
revenge of the man who hated all her family.

The man who had tied him mounted. "Get on."

Webb rode past Martha. She spoke to him very quietly.
"You dog," she said.

There was one consolation, Webb thought bitterly, as
he fell in with the others. Lute and Shorty, the only two
men who knew he had been ready to betray Bannister

were dead. With them out of the way, perhaps escape next time would be easier.

For escape he would. He had taken sides in this affair, whether he was wanted or not. He was a San Patricio man now, but due to be hated by them more than he was by his captors.

CHAPTER TWELVE

AFTER THE CATTLEMEN'S MEETING had broken up that afternoon, Mitch Budrow hunted out Tolleston, who was talking to some ranchers. He did not join the group on the bank steps, but waited patiently until he caught Tolleston's attention.

"You want me, Budrow?" Buck asked.

"If you got a minute," Mitch said diffidently. Tolleston excused himself from the group. "Well?" he said to Mitch.

"I'd like to write a letter and get it out on tonight's stage," Mitch told him. "I wondered if you'd be around long enough for me to do it."

"Letter?" Tolleston asked, and then smiled slightly. "A girl, Mitch."

Mitch grinned. "Yes, sir. I got a letter from her the other day and somehow I ain't had time to answer it."

"Go ahead," Buck told him. "I'll be in town a long while yet." He turned to go, then paused. "Be careful, Mitch. No word to her about what we've planned."

"Sure. She lives in Tucson, anyway. It's just about a few head of cattle we was aimin' to buy—her and me. She needed a little money."

"You got it?" Buck asked.

"I reckon."

Buck reached in his pocket and drew out a roll of bills. He peeled off some and handed them to Mitch. "Maybe that'll buy you a few more head, Mitch. That's for the work you've done."

Mitch looked at the money, speechless for the moment. Then he stammered, "I—I sure do thank you. That'll please her."

Buck ignored the thanks and returned to his conversation. Mitch pocketed the money and went down the street to the Territorial House, fighting a feeling of self-loathing. On his way he stopped in and bought two drinks and then crossed to the hotel. He felt better.

At the desk he got some stationery and some envelopes and went over to the writing table. In full detail, he wrote down the plans that he had been listening to all afternoon. It included the date of the planned raid on Bull Foot, the time, the men who were leading, the number to expect, the full plans of how the town would be burned. Finished, he folded the paper and put it in an envelope which he addressed to Tom Kean, telegrapher and freight agent at Bull Foot. In this he was following Bannister's orders. Then he addressed the second envelope to a fictitious name and address in Tuscon, stuffed the envelope with blank sheets of paper, and went out.

At the post office in Samuelson's Emporium, he bought stamps from Samuelson himself.

"How long you reckon it'd take to get a saddle up here from Tucson?" he asked Samuelson.

"A week," the storekeeper replied.

"That's what the company said. They said I should have it by now."

"Maybe it's been held up somewhere."

Mitch nodded and looked at his letter. "Is the name of that there freight agent in Bull Foot, Kean?"

"That's right."

Mitch stamped the letter then. "Maybe this'll wake him up," he said mildly. "I'll bet it's layin' in his back room right now."

Samuelson said likely it was, and took Mitch's two
letters. Then he looked around him and said in a low
voice, "That was mighty nice work, Budrow. You deserve a heap of credit for that."

Mitch said, "My fun is goin' to come tomorrow night,
I hope."

"Don't you worry about that," Samuelson said, and
they shook hands on it. Mitch left and went down to the
O. K. corral where he sat on a sack of oats and waited
patiently for Tolleston. He figured his back trail was
covered. He didn't feel like talking to Iron Hat Petty,
who sat in a back-tilted chair under the arch. Iron Hat
didn't feel like talking either, so they were both silent.
Mitch felt as if he never wanted to talk again.

He retained that feeling until the next afternoon.
Two hours before dusk, the ten riders of the Broken
Arrow, headed by Tolleston saddled up and headed in
the direction of Wagon Mound. There was a rank smell
of kerosene about them, which seemed to come from the
fat slickers tied on the cantle of each saddle. It had to
do with the Bull Foot raid. Every man was to carry a
sack of coal-oil-soaked rags wrapped in his slicker.

Until dark, the Broken Arrow riders avoided trails.
Then they took them because it was faster going. Two
hours after dark they had swung wide of Wagon Mound
and were headed for Belly Butte, the huge landmark that
lay almost on the county line.

Arriving at the west side of its base, they found riders
already gathered, and the stench of coal oil filled the air.
The men stood quietly by their horses, and Mitch could
not begin to count the number. But he figured roughly
that seventy men were in this posse. The leaders were
gathered together in the center of the band. Small dia-
monds of starlight glinted on carbines in saddle boots,
on guns on hips, on rows and rows of belted cartridges.

The talk was hushed, somber, and there was none of the usual joking and horseplay which is always present when cowboys meet.

Tolleston was greeted quietly.

"You timed it about right," Hasker said.

"Everybody here?"

"They will be any time now. We had to leave some of the boys in town to yarn with the stage driver, so it wouldn't look funny."

They reviewed their duties. Eventually part of the posse was to be split up into four groups of roughly ten men each. Each group was to enter town from a different direction. They were to travel the streets slowly, smothering any premature alarm that the townsfolk would give. The rest were divided up into small squads which would travel the alleys and fire the buildings. Eight men carefully picked—and Mitch was among those eight—were to cover the two barrooms, four men to a saloon. They were to hold the customers at bay until the fire had a start. By that time the town would be in flames, and panic would be in the streets. Then the four groups were to ride to the center of town and shoot up the long main street. Any man that fired on them was to be hunted down and exterminated, while the others were freeing saddle horses from the hitch-racks and driving them off.

Then, once the limit of town was reached, the whole band would ride hell-for-leather for Wake Bannister's Dollar spread. A few men would drop back to cover the back trail. The plan seemed reasonable, all the way around.

When the last arrivals were present, everyone mounted and the long ride to Bull Foot began. Opinion was that, by ways of an old drive trail long in disuse but remembered by most of the older men present, it would take four hours to reach Bull Foot. This would put them in close to one o'clock. They did not miss it far. The ride was swift, businesslike, and these men kept the same grim silence, except to curse a horse now and then. As they traveled deeper into Wintering, the leaders went a little slower. The knowledge that discovery here would mean death tended to make them wary.

Passing over a long bench where they clung to the shadow of the bordering trees, Miles Kindry said to Tolleston, "I used to brand down off yonder by the creek."

"It's a nice range," Tolleston said quietly. "If this goes through, you'll get it back. Ted Bannister's on it now, ain't he?"

"One of that coyote clan," Miles replied. In spite of the fat which made him hulk awkwardly in the saddle, in spite of the years that had passed since he laid claim to this range, there was a passion in his speech that might have been a key to the feelings of all these old-timers tonight.

Starlight and dust and horse lather and saddle creak enveloped Mitch, but he neither saw nor smelled nor heard them. In the note which he had sent to Kean yesterday he had added a footnote. It had told Bannister, almost apologetically, that he, Mitch Budrow, would be one of the men who were to hold up the Melodian. Would Bannister please inform the ambushers that he would be wearing a red neckerchief, so they might know him?

Now, he didn't know. He could almost feel fear creeping up on him, not to be banished. He knew his work for Bannister had been completed, and completed well. But now that Bannister had no more use for him, wouldn't he plan to get rid of him? After all, Mitch was the sole man outside of Hugo Meeker who knew the part Bannister had played in manufacturing this ambush.

To play safe, Bannister might wipe out all evidence, and Mitch bulked large as evidence—and the wrong kind. The longer he rode, the more insistent this thought became.

When the posse reined up on the timbered hogbacks that lay to the east of Bull Foot, the lights of town were easily visible ahead and below. Bull Foot, since the day it was established, had been a tolerant as well as prosperous town. Settled in the wide fold of hills through which the railway managed to snake up from the south, it was larger than Wagon Mound. Its two main streets, crossing each other in the center of the town, were wider. The stores were more numerous, and they were painted. Behind the main street paralleling the tracks and on the shorter cross streets lay the courthouse, a two-story, white frame affair with jigsaw cupolas.

The town itself, in spite of the hour, was lighted. Some of the stores still held customers. The saloons were booming, and there were lights at the feed corral two doors north of the Melodian.

The leaders moved up in a circle for consultation.

"It looks like we've done it," Wes Anders said, quiet exultation in his voice. He had once been the largest stockholder in the solid-looking bank which squatted on the four corners below.

"Yes," Tolleston said, satisfaction in his voice. "Hasker, you're taking your men around west and down past the courthouse. You better start now."

Hasker had his men grouped. They left and followed the hogbacks to the south and were swallowed by darkness. The others split up, too, until only the eight who were to hold up the two saloons were left.

Mac said to them, "Well, my four, come along. And remember, boys, don't gallop in and don't sneak in. Just ride in."

Mitch joined his band. It was to ride in from the south. They sloped down to the road, crossed the tracks and turned up the main street. Mitch was alert for any sign that would give the ambush away, but he could find none. A scattering of people were on the streets, and the huge Bannister Mercantile was lighted and still held some customers. For a moment Mitch wondered if maybe Bannister hadn't received his letter. His spine started to crawl at the thought.

And then he looked up beneath his hat brim at the second story of the Wintering Hotel. Every window there was dark, every window open. Yes, Bannister had got the note all right.

In front of the Melodian the four of them dismounted.

"Watch your ties," Mike Sutton, a Seven A cowboy and their leader, said.

The din from the Melodian was loud and sustained, a commingling of talk, shrill laughter, glass clink, monotonous calls of the faro dealers, shuffling feet, and the insipid grind of a piano.

Mitch's hand fumbled as he tied his reins to the tie rail, so that the others had to wait for him.

Once on the sidewalk, he said, "This is a mighty big place for four of us to take."

The puncher he addressed turned a cold, hard face to him.

"You want to pull out?"

Mitch shook his head and managed to return the man's stare. "Did I say I did?"

"All right," Sutton said, and drew two six-guns. The others, including Mitch, did the same. As Sutton had his hand out to push open the batwing doors, a drunken cow-puncher staggered out the other half of the door.

Sutton shoved him back into the room and stepped in, the others behind him. Mitch was last, and his face was plaster-gray. Sutton put a shot over the customers' heads into the bar mirror, and the din stopped as suddenly as if it had been a thread cut by a knife.

Sutton looked over the crowd, his guns covering them. "Back up from the bar, folks," he drawled in the silence. "You barkeeps stay on deck and hoist your hands."

There was a general milling away from the bar. Suddenly somebody said in a low voice which carried clear over the room, "Ain't them San Patricio cowboys?"

"Right," Sutton replied. "San Patricio cowboys just rode over for their pay check."

It was quiet again. Mitch's hands were wet with sweat against his gun butts. He looked over the heads of the crowd. And then he saw something which yanked the breath out of his throat. On the back balcony, which was stacked with empty beer kegs, he saw a movement. Slowly, counting them, he saw the barrels of six shotguns nose through between the beer kegs and steady themselves.

With a strangled cry, Mitch turned and ran the two steps to the door. Even as he turned, he saw the puncher nearest him grab for him, cursing.

And then the shotguns blasted out in ragged peroration. Mitch felt a spatter of buckshot slap into the door, felt his ear snipped, and then he was outside, running upstreet.

From far upstreet he heard a mighty blast of gunfire. That would be Mac's outfit getting it at the Running Iron. Mitch paused, looking behind him.

He could see a group of horsemen paused at the four corners. Even while he watched, another group joined them, and still a third. People began to pour out of the saloon. The horsemen let out a yell and started down the street.

Suddenly a rifle cracked across the street and a slug buried itself in the board by Mitch's head. He moaned and started to run.

And then the heavens opened up. A furious concert of gunfire rolled out, and Mitch dived for an opening between two buildings. He paused just long enough to look back. All four groups of the San Patricio riders were galloping down the street, caught between two lines of gunfire. The whole town of Bull Foot seemed suddenly to appear from behind the false fronts of the stores and rain down leaden death into the street.

Riderless horses galloped by. The vanguard of the raiders passed Mitch now, their guns booming. Miles Kindry's big bulk was bent over his saddle horn, his reins trailing. Another rider slammed into his horse, and Miles toppled out of the saddle. A horse reared and five blind riders piled into it and they went down in a moil of dust and screams, and the fire was directed toward it.

From the back alley, now, Mitch heard the racket of shots. That would mean that the men who were firing the buildings had been ambushed.

Mitch shrank against the building, his eyes wild with panic. The street before him was a shambles. The San Patricio raiders were not even shooting now. To a man they lay along the necks of their horses, Indian fashion, trying desperately to get out of town. Crippled horses spilled their riders; there was the raucous voice of a puncher cursing wildly as he tried to yank a down rider up onto his saddle. Two men on the Wintering Hotel roof opened up. The cursing rider, in the act of giving his friend a hand up, raised up in his stirrups and the down rider pulled him over. Before the horse had a chance to shy, its front legs buckled and it, too, went down.

Mitch watched it to the bitter end, until the last San Patricio rider either escaped or was whipped out of the saddle and rolled in a cloud of dust.

Then self-preservation took hold of Mitch with a vengeance. He suddenly remembered that someone had driven a shot at him from across the street—at him, who had made all this possible. Without even forming the words in his mind, he knew that that shot had been fired at Bannister's orders. He could imagine the word being passed around the whole town: "Get the man with the red neckerchief!"

Mitch whipped it off and stuffed it in his pocket and then turned toward the alley. He could hear men running on the board walk, their cries rising over the screams of dying men and horses.

Mitch halted at the back of the building. Men were back there. He could hear them calling to each other.

Casting frantically about him, he saw a barrel under an eavespout at the corner. He leaped for it, climbed its rim, and dropped inside. There was a foot of water in it, so cold it took his breath away, but he crouched down, fighting to still his laboring breath.

Here it is, he thought with a kind of frantic calmness. *I've been dodgin' it for two years. And here it is.*

He heard men shouting, heard them pound past him, the earth shaking gently beneath him. Then silence. He did not move.

Suddenly, a voice came clearly to him: "I tell you he went in here. Hell, didn't I shoot at him?"

"But he's gone," another voice said.

"He won't get far then. He's likely been cut down already."

"All right. Let it ride that way."

The first speaker cursed. "Let it ride?" he echoed. "Hell, do you know whose orders it was to get him?"

"Sure."

"All right, go get your drink. I'm lookin'."

There were footsteps. Then the second voice, fading now, but not so faint that Mitch didn't hear it plainly, said, "Can't we tie a red handkerchief on one of these dead rannies and say we thought it was him?"

Mitch didn't feel any surprise at this. It was as if somebody had spoken what was inevitable and what he had known in his own mind. He crouched there, a kind of stupefaction soothing him.

This, he was thinking, *is the end of the trail that began two years ago when I strangled that honkytonk girl.*

And then the panic returned and he was afraid again. He wanted to live, and he didn't care how. But the fear in him was not so strong that he could not see two things clearly. If he got out of here and rode to Tolleston again, he would be killed. His cowardice there in the saloon would be the pointing finger which would lead to a hang-noose death. If he stayed here in Wintering County, Bannister would hunt him out and kill him. If he left Wintering County, there were those United States marshals, particularly the one from Tucson. For some months he had known peace from them. But now, if he was always to live in terror of them, he would rather be dead. And Bannister would be sure to write, giving them his trail.

Mitch crouched there shivering. No, the best thing to do was to go to Bannister. Folks said Bannister never killed a man by his own hand. Go to Bannister, beg for mercy, for work, stay by him, never leave him until he gave his promise of safety. To Mitch this idea had nothing of the daring about it. It meant life.

Waiting there was almost pleasant then, because he had hope. After another fifteen minutes in which he heard nothing but shouts and commotion on the street, he climbed out of the barrel and slunk down the alley. Halfway down it, a horse nickered. Mitch struck a light and saw a big bay standing there, a man lying face down beside the trailing reins. Mitch recognized him, recognized the horse. It was a Broken Arrow hand who owed him seven dollars. Apparently the man had tried to run for his horse, for in one hand was a swab of oil-soaked rags, in the other his gun.

Mitch let the match die and took the horse, leading it down the alley. When he came to the cross street he boldly turned into it and rode out of town, not answering questions the townspeople on the walks called to him.

Once in the clear, he rode frantically for the Dollar spread. When he arrived, he rode into the plaza. Some Mexicans stopped him and asked him what had happened.

"*Nada*," Mitch said wearily. "Nothing."

He put his horse up in Mooney's corral and then made his way through the dark to Bannister's office. The door was locked. He hunted around the front of the blacksmith shop for a scrap of iron and, finding one, broke the lock on the door. The office was dark. He didn't light a lamp.

He sat down in one of the chairs to wait, his eyes sleepless, knowing that if he went to sleep before he saw Wake Bannister, he would never wake.

CHAPTER THIRTEEN

T WENTY-TWO MISSING OUT OF seventy," Will Wardecker said gently into the night. "We were lucky."

All around him he could hear the labored breathing of blown horses, could smell gun smoke and blood. The forms around him he could not distinguish, but occasionally he could hear the caught breath of a man trying to hide pain.

"Buck Tolleston," Wardecker called.

"Yes," a voice answered from beside him.

Before Wardecker could speak, a puncher out in the night said, "My horse is blowed. I'm ridin' on! They'll be after us!"

"Stay here!" Buck ordered sharply. "They won't follow us! They don't have to." Then he said to Wardecker in a weary, dead voice, "Who's here?"

"Better ask." The sheriff said.

Tolleston called, "Hasker."

"I got through."

"Kindry."

No answer.

"Bindloss."

No answer.

"Anders, Pillsbury, Dale, Sweetser."

Sweetser answered.

And so it went. Only five out of seven names called answered. At the end of it, Tolleston, sick and miserable, said, "Let's ride. This is no place for us."

Once under way, Wardecker turned his horse in beside Tolleston's. There was that comradeship between them which only years can bring, and tonight Buck Tolleston needed it more than he ever had before.

Wardecker said, "Who was it sold us, Buck?"

"I don't know," Buck answered after a while. "Whoever it was knew everything we planned and how to nail us down."

"I hope he's dead," Wardecker said. "I hope he has been shot in his guts and stays in agony for hours."

Tolleston said nothing, and presently Wardecker said, "No, I don't, either. I can't imagine anything worse than havin' to live with that crime on your mind. I hope he's alive."

Buck only sighed. Behind all the grief he felt over lost friends, over the ruin and desolation that this night would mean, loomed one fact that Buck was secretly ashamed of, but which he could no more deny than he could deny he was alive and safe. And that fact was that Bannister had won, finally and irrevocably.

Wardecker understood a little of what Buck was thinking. He said without any reproof, "Well, Buck, I reckon it took this to prove we're second fiddle."

"Yes," Tolleston said, not believing it.

The rest of the long night they rode in silence. The sunrise which caught them just over the county line did not help any. Some time in the night, a Chain Link rider had dropped out of his saddle without being heard. Almost all of them had gunshot wounds, some bad, some not serious. Most were gray of face, exhausted, beaten. Lou Hasker's right pants leg was stiff with blood, and he was not riding a Chain Link branded horse. Somehow, in that massacre when his horse was shot from under him, he had managed to catch another and ride free. His hard young face was pinched and wooden, and the old confidence seemed drained out of him, Tolleston noticed.

Young Sweetser rode as if in a trance. But the bulk of the casualties had been borne by the punchers, as was always the case in range wars. A hard, loyal lot, they had sold their lives for a wage. Buck couldn't help but think of Mac. He of course, was dead, killed in the shooting which started the fight.

Buck hung his head in shame and weariness, too numb to hate, even. He was riding in the rear of the group when they rounded the curve in the road that should have put them in sight of Wagon Mound, but he did not look up.

The first hint of anything wrong was the bitter wild of a man up front. Then Buck noticed that these men had stopped. He reined around those ahead and walked his horse until he had a clear view of the shallow plain on which Wagon Mound was situated.

Ahead of him was a smoking heap of ashes, one long building—the brick bank—standing upright. The cottonwoods which had shaded part of the town were shriveled and sere.

Something died in Buck Tolleston then. He turned haunted eyes to Wardecker. When he tried to speak he couldn't, for a growing rage was throttling him. Savagely he rammed his spurs into his tired horse and galloped into town at the head of the weary band.

People—mostly women and children—were on the streets at the four corners, and Buck pulled up in a moil of dust to survey the sight. Everything was destroyed: stores, homes, buildings, corrals, everything that was inflammable—which meant the whole town. It was as level as the plain around it, except for the blackened fingers of a few stone chimneys which poked up from the charred ruins.

Iron Hat Petty hobbled up to the horsemen. "They met you, I reckon," Iron Hat said.

And then a girl broke through the ranks of watchers.

"Dad! Dad!" she cried.

It was Martha. Buck took her in his arms and let her cry, holding her close, stroking her hair. Other women now were hunting their men, and those that did not find them were hearing out the story of the massacre in Bull Foot. Buck buried his face in Martha's hair and closed his eyes.

Presently she looked up at him. "Can you stand any more of this, dad—more news that will hurt?"

Buck only looked at her.

"The spread was fired last night by Bannister. All the big places were. The Seven A, the Wagon Hammer, Pillsbury's, Winterhovens—all of them. Burned to the ground."

Buck took it without a change of expression. A man can absorb only so much shock. The others were like him, too, unable to comprehend at first the extent of their loss.

Later, Buck took Iron Hat to one side. "What happened, Iron Hat?"

"Just what you see. Bannister rode into town with half a hundred riders and took over the town. Warned all the women and kids out of the houses and stores. Wally Hubbel thought he'd fort up in the sheriff's office and fight, so they just burned it down on top of him. Outside of that, I don't reckon there was a man killed. They drove all the horses in town off. Then they split and started ridin' over the county. Folks—mostly women-folks—have been driftin' in all day with news of what they done. Most of the big ranches is burned clean to the ground, all except the Chain Link and yours. They was made of stone and wouldn't take fire, but they burned everything around it." Iron Hat recited this in his dull, flat voice. He needed whisky. There was none to be had.

Buck walked away from him. Wardecker had called a meeting of the men as they were resting in front of the bank.

"First thing we got to do is feed these women and kids," Wardecker said. "I'll need three men besides myself to rustle up a couple of steers and haze 'em into town. Some of you others ought to dig around in the ashes and see if there's any flour left over in Samuelson's cellar. As soon as we get somethin' to eat, we can take stock."

By afternoon a rude camp of sorts had been made in the street at the four corners. Beefs had been killed and skinned out, and the camp was fed. Children were sleeping. The women had taken over and there was some semblance of order. Again the men lying exhausted before the bank were wakened, and again Wardecker assumed charge.

"You'll all want to go back to your places," he began, "but first we ought to have some idea of what's in the future." He turned to Tolleston. "Buck, what do you think?"

"Build up the place again," Buck said immediately. "We got our stock, accordin' to what I've heard. We did it fifteen years ago. We can do it again."

Frank Winterhoven, a gnarled, silent man, who lived over west, spoke then. "Not me, Buck. I'm pullin' out. I ain't blamin' you nor any man for what happened, but I've had a bellyful. I got two youngsters, a few horses, a couple of wagons, and plenty of cattle, but I owe notes that'll wipe me out, and I don't aim to fight over a dead horse. I'm pullin' out."

Several other men seconded him. Many of the big ranches in the county did not have a man left to run them. Most of them had borrowed money or saved it, and the bank robbery had cleaned them out. Buck could understand this, and he respected it, but he did not agree with it.

"I'm stayin'," he said quietly. "All my money's gone, my place is burned and the town's burned, but I'm stayin'. This country has kept me for fifteen years. I reckon it'll keep me another fifteen." He gestured south, and said quietly, "As for that outfit, I'll square myself with 'em one day. Time enough."

But the majority of them were apathetic, beaten. The younger men wanted to leave, all except those who were so small that Bannister had not bothered to burn them. Privately they thought Buck old, a madman too set in his ways ever to change. They looked to Lou Hasker for advice. He refused to give it.

"You got to settle that for yourselves. I don't know what I'll do. When I get this leg healed up and see what's happened to my outfit, and figure what the chances of stayin' here and makin' a livin' are, then I'll tell you. But don't ask me."

So it went. Some joined in with Buck, others reserved their opinions, but many of them, the majority, intended to leave.

"As far as I'm concerned, Wardecker," Winterhoven said, "you can arrange for a sheriff's sale as soon as it's handy. And that goes for most of us. The sooner I pull out the better, and I reckon some others feel the same way about it."

"You're makin' a mistake, Frank," Buck said.

"I've made too many a'ready," Frank said grimly. "One more won't hurt."

CHAPTER FOURTEEN

Bannister's own group of riders was the last to return. It was far past sun-up when they rode into the plaza. A look at the place assured Bannister it had not been touched, and therefore that the ambush in Bull Foot had been a success. He looked across at Meeker and smiled a little, and then his face sobered.

"Go get those Montana men and bring them to me, along with Cousins."

He rode over and left his horse at the corral, then walked over to his office. Symonds was working at his forge and looked up in time to see Bannister's cheery wave and return it. Bannister opened the door, and found a man standing in the room.

He peered sharply at the man, adjusting his eyes to the gloom of the room, and then drawled, "Why, good morning, Mitch."

"Morning," Mitch replied.

Bannister walked across to his desk, saying, "Well, how did it go in Bull Foot?"

"Just like you planned it," Mitch replied calmly. "They rode into it, and I reckon a lot of 'em was killed."

Bannister looked up from the papers on his desk. "Who?"

"Kindry, Anders, Bindloss, I seen go down. The street was full of 'em."

"Not Tolleston?"

"No. I didn't see him, leastways."

"He'd better not be dead," Bannister said grimly. "I'm not through with him yet." He sat down, and Mitch stood there, his face utterly calm.

"Wake," Mitch said quietly. Bannister looked up, surprised to hear his name in Mitch's mouth. His eyes were hard, but contrived to look pleasant.

Mitch said huskily, "Call 'em off, will you? I'll never sell out on you! Gosh, look what I've done for you already! Look what you can hold over my head. I want to live, Wake! I got to!"

"What are you talkin' about?" Bannister drawled mildly, settling back in his chair.

Mitch swallowed. "About me. They're tryin' to kill me. I know because I heard 'em huntin' me in town when I run."

"Heard who?"

"I dunno. But they was huntin' a man with a red neckerchief. Aimin' to shoot him. They said it was your—"

Just then footsteps sounded outside. Bannister rose and said sharply, "Get in that room, Mitch. And don't come out till I tell you! Quick now!"

Mitch obediently dived for the door of the adjoining room and slipped inside just as the front door opened. Bannister was hunched over his desk.

When he looked up the three Montana men, stonyfaced and wary-looking, were standing beside Webb, whose head was mottled with blood.

"What's happened, boss?" Perry Warren asked. He was the least communicative of them all, Webb had learned, a truculent, nervous man of thirty or so, with a vicious, thin mouth and an irritable temper. Webb had long since concluded that if Lute ever dropped out, Warren would head the others. He slouched now, hands on hips, hat on the back of his head. He was wearing a vest, mostly from habit, since the day was warm.

Bannister leaned back in his chair and regarded them coldly.

"I don't know why I bother keeping you three around," he said quietly. "Maybe I hadn't ought to."

A small shadow of fear crept into Warren's eyes. "What's the trouble?"

Bannister said, "You boys thought you'd ride out on a private raiding party, didn't you?"

Perry glanced obliquely at Webb and then drawled, "You got us wrong, Bannister. The three of us was in the bunk house all night like Meeker said."

"What about the other two—and Cousins, here?"

"They went," Warren said, "but not us. No, sir. They tried to toll us in on it, but we wasn't havin' any. I know when I'm well off, even if them boys didn't." He gestured to Webb. "Cousins here couldn't help hisself. He never wanted to go, but they made him, because he knowed his way around over there." Now he turned to Webb. "That right, fella?"

Without ever putting it in words, Warren had made Webb a proposition. If Webb would not tell Bannister they had talked this over among themselves and almost fought for the privilege of going, then Warren would not tell Bannister that it had been Webb who had suggested it.

Webb nodded. "That's about it, Bannister. I didn't have a choice." He jerked his head toward the others. "These three voted it down and we went on playin' poker. Pretty soon Lute took me out to get a bottle. Shorty drifted out later. Then they went over and got horses, tied me on mine, and told me to take them over into San Patricio."

"So you took them to Tolleston's?"

Webb shrugged. "It's the only outfit I knew. I'd rather take 'em than get shot in the back."

Bannister sat back and studied them with quiet arrogance. He knew they were lying. It annoyed him mildly, not because he disapproved of what they had done, but because they had disobeyed him, and that, in a hired inferior, was something Bannister would not put up with. Then he turned to his desk and pulled a letter out from under the mass of papers. Opening it, he glanced at it, then took up his pencil, erased a word, and put another in its place. All the time he was doing this, he was talking to the four men waiting:

"The whole pack of you are lying. If you want the truth, it's this. You saw all this preparation going on yesterday and you snooped around until you found it was to be a raid. Since you make a living off things like that, you didn't want to be left out. Some of you might have been cautious, but most of you wanted to risk it. You got caught. You all had orders, and you'll take your punishment for disobeying them." Here he paused and folded the letter again and shoved it back in the heap of papers. Then he turned to them.

"We've got something that passes for a respectable jail around here. I'll let you sit it out in there until you come to me with the truth. I never hire a liar—or if I do, I take care that I can see through his lies. Take them out, Hugo."

"All of 'em?" Hugo asked.

"Yes. Cousins can be guarded by Britt's paid guards while they're all in jail," Bannister said dryly.

The Montana men settled into a surly silence. Perry Warren shrugged. Webb's face was stupid, as expressionless as he could make it while Hugo herded them outside. Directly across from the blacksmith's shop was the end room of the wing. It had barred windows, a heavy door and served as the jail. Webb and his companions were ordered into it, and the door locked behind them.

As soon as Meeker left with his prisoners, Bannister,

smiling a little, called, "Come out, Mitch."

Mitch did. He had calmed down a little during his wait, but his eyes were filled with the same desperation.

Bannister said kindly, "Sit down, Mitch. That was Cousins. I didn't want him to see you."

When Mitch was seated, Bannister said, "Now tell me this again. You think someone is trying to get you because I gave the orders. Is that it?"

"That's right," Mitch said huskily. He told of hiding in the rain barrel. At this moment Meeker came in and seated himself, listening.

Mitch went on earnestly: "Then I heard them arguin'. One man wanted to quit, and the other man didn't. So the second jasper says, 'Let's tie a red handkerchief around a dead man and claim we thought it was him!' But the other man wouldn't." Mitch leaned forward in his chair, his face wet with perspiration. "Bannister, if you're goin' to do it, do it now!"

Bannister simply stared at him in mild unbelief. Then he started to laugh, and the chuckles seemed to come from deep in him. He leaned forward and patted Mitch's knee.

"I think I understand," he said. "I'm sure I do."

He hunted among the papers on his desk, and after some pretense of rummaging, drew forth the letter he had put back only a few minutes ago. Unfolding it, he studied it carefully, then he showed it to Mitch. "You wrote this, didn't you?"

Mitch glanced at it. "Sure. That's the plan I sent from Wagon Mound."

"Look at the postscript," Bannister said. "Did you write that?"

Mitch read the postscript. His face lost its tension and in its place was an expression of bewilderment. He looked up at Bannister. "But I never wrote that," he said earnestly. "This has been changed. Here it says, 'Miles

Kindry will be wearing a red neckerchief, so you'll know.'
I never wrote that! I wrote, 'I'll be wearin' a red neckerchief, so you'll know.' " Mitch looked at Bannister and
then at Meeker.

Bannister said, "Yes. I read there that Miles Kindry
would be wearin' a red neckerchief. I thought you wrote
it. I wanted Miles Kindry dead, so I gave orders to cut
down on the man wearin' that neckerchief."

Mitch still looked puzzled.

Hugo cleared his throat. "Hell, that's easy. The man
that changed that letter wants Mitch Budrow dead. They
figured he'd get shot instead of Miles Kindry."

Mitch asked quietly, "Who knows me here?"

Bannister frowned, looking from Hugo to Mitch.
Suddenly he said softly, "Sure, that's it." Now he looked
at Mitch. "Kean, the station agent, must have been doing
a little bounty hunting, Mitch."

"I don't get it."

Bannister leaned forward. "You sent your letter about
the San Patricio plans to Kean, didn't you? He was to
give them to me."

Mitch nodded.

"And you signed your name, didn't you?"

"Sure," Mitch said.

Bannister spread his hands. "All right, Kean has had
a reward dodger with your name and your picture on
the station bulletin board. Likely, as soon as he read your
letter and knew you were coming on the raid, he figured
he'd collect bounty money on you. So he changes your
letter to read 'Miles Kindry will be wearing a red neckerchief, so you'll know.' He knew I'd make a special play
for Miles. But if his plan worked, my men would get you,
then Kean would step in and collect bounty money on
you." Bannister leaned back in his chair. "I'll set a few
things right with him, you can bet, Mitch."

Mitch relaxed. He stared down at the floor like a man

who has been reprieved from death and who is dumb with relief and gratitude. Bannister only looked over Mitch's head to Hugo and there was unspoken praise in Hugo's eyes.

Bannister cleared his throat. He did not want to treat this as any more than a mistake, so he thought Mitch should be only mildly reassured.

"Hugo," he ordered, "you send a man down to see Kean and post him straight on this. Better yet, stop in and see him yourself when you go in today. Also, make sure all over again that all those reward notices about Mitch are taken down."

"Sure," Hugo said carelessly.

"As for you, Mitch, you'd better get some sleep. I'll have a check made out for you when you wake up." He smiled fondly. "I just want to say this, Mitch. I think you did a wonderful job with this. Not only that, but I'm going to keep you here now. Hugo could split his work with another man and still have a lot to do. Not the ranch work, understand, but the other work—my private work. I think you'll do it well."

Mitch dragged himself to his feet. He was so weak with relief that he could only mumble his thanks. As he was going out, Bannister said, "Better bunk at Mooney's now, Mitch. It's safer."

When Mitch was gone, Bannister sat back in his chair and cursed softly. Suddenly he said to Hugo, "Who was supposed to get him?"

"Two of the boys. Good men, I thought."

"Pay them off and tell them to get out of the country!"

"Is that wise?" Hugo asked.

Bannister was about to reply, then he closed his mouth and smiled slightly. "All right. Keep them. I'll have a chance to tend to them."

Hugo said, "What about Mitch? He'll be asleep over there now."

"Not now," Bannister said thoughtfully. "Not around here, either. He's had a scare. Maybe we can still use him."

"Be careful, Wake."

"I will. But not now."

CHAPTER FIFTEEN

At the Broken Arrow, camp was made the first night under the huge cottonwoods, back of the house. Buck had already talked to Mrs. Partridge, Charley, and the four remaining hands. He had told them that they need not stay with him if they wished to leave, but Buck Tolleston bred a strange loyalty. They all wanted to stay, quarters or no quarters, and were willing to wait for their pay.

While Martha and Mrs. Partridge got a meal together from the food stored in the fruit cellar, Buck looked around. The barns and corrals and wagon sheds and everything in them was burned, of course. The house still stood, but every bit of wood that went into it was burned. The roof was off, the interior gutted, and nothing remained but a solid, blackened shell.

Buck had always considered this place temporary, little more than a camp which he would live in until he had taken his old place—Wake Bannister's Dollar spread—away from him. But now that it was in ruins he realized what deep affection he had held for it. Here was where his girl had grown to womanhood, where he had spent some of the best years of his life.

He returned to camp under the trees and ate supper. There was little need for talk. All were thinking of the task ahead of them. They turned in after supper and slept soundly.

Next morning, Martha did what little could be done around the place before the work of construction began again. Day before yesterday she had ridden out to meet Britt, and he had not appeared. Of course all this stupid and bloody fighting which they both hated could have made it impossible for him to meet her, but she wanted to see him. The chances of their ever being married seemed more hopeless now, in the light of what had happened yesterday and the night before. It was a wall that stood between them, growing ever higher, for Martha could not forgive this cruel and senseless ravaging of the Broken Arrow. Still less could she forgive the mass murder that had taken place in Bull Foot. And, try as she might, she could not forget that the man behind all this was Britt Bannister's father.

All in all, she was bewildered. She wanted someone to talk to, someone with a calm head. Too, she knew that marriage with Britt was out of the question for years now, since her father would need her help. And the thought of Buck Tolleston ever resigning himself to her marriage with a Bannister was fantastic, in the light of what had happened.

Another thing she wanted to ask Britt. How was it that this Webb Cousins, whom Britt had promised to guard and keep, had been in the vanguard of these raiders? Had they turned loose every mad dog in Wintering County? With a little shudder she thought of the two dead men, Lute and Shorty, who still lay in the wagon box over where the barn used to be. This morning their graves were being dug.

She looked at the house, and the sight of it depressed her. Turning away from it, she strolled up the hill. Once on the ridge, she sat down in the shade of a cedar and relaxed. Presently she noticed off to her right an object which she could not identify. Curiosity finally compelled her to rise and go over to it. It was a length of rope, one

end of which was sawed raggedly. Beside it was a shard
from a broken bottle. They both lay near the tracks of
a horse. Picking up the rope, Martha noticed something
like dried blood on it.

She dropped it, wondering about it. Looking closer,
she could see the tracks of where a man had dismounted
from his horse, and where he had gone over to where two
other horses stood. Then the tracks turned and headed
down the hill. They were far apart, indicating that the
man was in a hurry. Curious, Martha followed them.
They took her down to the corner of where the wagon
shed used to stand, and then they headed for the house.
The man had been running then, for only the toes of his
boots left tracks and they were deep in the dirt and far
apart. She went on. At the corner of the house they
paused, and then there were other marks rounding the
corner, new marks. It took her several minutes to puzzle
this out, but she got the clue. They were hand prints in
the dirt. She could see them in several places where they
had not been blotted out by the raiders' boot marks.

These hand prints and the print of a man's knees, followed the line of the house until they came to where the
porch had been. She saw, too, where a rock had been
moved from its place, but she could not find the rock.

Standing there, she tried to piece all this together.

Three horses had been up on the hill. A piece of
bloody rope, cut raggedly. Of course! Cut with the bottle.
But cut from where? And then she remembered Webb
Cousins, standing in the door of the house talking to the
man who was demanding the combination of the safe
from her. When Webb had made his threat, holstered his
gun, she had noticed his bleeding wrists. "Then he was
brought over here tied on his horse!"

She began to wonder why. If he had been tied on his
horse, then he would have to wait until those other two
were out of sight to free himself. That chance would be

supplied when the other two were talking to her. Then it was Webb Cousin's tracks that she had followed. He had run down to the house and crawled from the corner of it to the porch.

Why?

She tried to remember that night. There had been a man standing in the door, training a gun on them while the other man walked across the room. But the man in the door wasn't Cousins. Then how did Cousins get there —and get a gun, for wasn't he a prisoner? Or was he?

She stood there, trying to puzzle it out. Then she walked across the corral lot, hunting for Charley. She saw him and another man digging **up** near the edge of the timber and set out to walk the distance.

Charley ceased work when she approached. He glanced at the bulk under a tarp off under the trees and came over to her.

"Charley, what happened the night we got burned out? Where did you come in?"

"I was asleep in the bunk house," Charley said slowly, rubbing his bald head. "I heard the racket of a lot of horses comin'. I knowed it couldn't be Buck comin' back, but I didn't know exactly what it was. I got my guns and headed for the house. I seen the light. Comin' up close to the porch, I stumbled on a man lyin' there. Then I looked up and seen that rider whippin' out a gun and before I could do anything, he'd shot. Then I cut down on him. You know the rest. Them riders came up and you made me give up my gun."

"I know. But you say you stumbled over a man. Which man?"

Charley jerked his thumb toward the tarp. "One of them."

"Was he shot?"

Charley shook his head. "I don't reckon. His head was bashed in."

That would account for the rock, Martha thought. Cousins had used it as a weapon. He had knocked this man in the head, grabbed his weapon, and killed the other man. She thanked Charley and turned away.

Walking back, she tried to remember what Cousins had said that night. When the first man said to give him a hand, Cousins had said the only hand he would get was a filled one. That was a threat to kill him, and he had. But why? So he could loot the safe? For the first time since that night, she began to wonder.

Her thoughts were disturbed by seeing two riders headed up the road to the house. One was a woman. It was probably Mrs. Anders come over to offer help or ask for it. Martha hurried ahead, feeling a deep sympathy for this woman whose husband was dead and whose home had been burned.

It was Mrs. Anders, a gray-haired gentlewoman in a man's rough clothes. Her face was lifeless, and she did not have the usual smile and cheery word she always gave to Martha. She had come over to borrow food, she said, until one of their hands could butcher out a beef. The hands had stayed in town last night to help straighten things up.

Mrs. Partridge went over to get some food and the Seven A Chinese cook went with her to get it.

Mrs. Anders looked at the house and shook her head. "You were lucky, my dear," she said to Martha. "Our house was log. It was burned level."

"We were lucky," Martha said.

Mrs. Anders said nothing for a while, then asked, "Did the whole crowd ride over here?"

"Yes. Wake Bannister and Hugo Meeker and more than twenty riders."

"And not that young whelp, Britt Bannister?" Mrs. Anders asked.

Martha kept her gaze on the house and did not answer

until she had control of herself.

"No, I don't think so. I don't think I know him."

Mrs. Anders laughed shortly. "If you ever saw him, you would. He's twice the devil his father is."

Martha asked casually, "Why do you say that? Do you know him?"

"Know him?" Mrs. Anders echoed bitterly. "I should think so. I had all our provisions down in the adobe well house. He ordered his men to go and haul them up and dump them in the fire. Every bit of food we had on the place. He even wanted to throw the saddles on the corral poles into the barn fire, but Hugo Meeker wouldn't let him."

Martha's spine grew cold. She could not trust herself to talk immediately. Then she thought that Mrs. Anders must be mistaken, that she was thinking of someone else.

Martha said slowly then, "I'd heard Bannister's boy— is Britt his name?—didn't share his father's views. I heard he kept out of this quarrel."

"He's a Bannister," Mrs. Anders said grimly. "He was there. I heard him named, time and again. I heard him call Wake Bannister 'dad.' Even if I hadn't, I could've told. He has the same face, the same manner about him."

Martha said no more. When Mrs. Partridge returned with the food, Mrs. Anders and her cook rode off. Still Martha sat there, her face pale. Britt was one of these raiders—Britt, who had laughed at this feud, who shared her hatred for it, and for useless bloodshed and killing. No, there was a mistake somewhere. Either Mrs. Anders was wrong or else Britt had changed, and Martha could not believe that of Britt. Still, something kept telling her, he had not come to meet her since he took Cousins away.

Martha caught a horse and rode out that afternoon. She waited at their meeting place until dusk, her mind in turmoil. Something inside her ached. When she returned that night, Buck was not home yet. As soon as Martha had pretended to eat her supper, she said she was going to ride.

Once in the saddle, she headed for the Talbots' shack over east on the edge of the Roan Creek bottom lands. The Talbots were squatters, tolerated by her father because Talbot had a large family and few cattle and rode line for the Broken Arrow three days a week.

There, in the dimly lighted shack, she was greeted by Talbot himself. She explained she had to write a letter, and that since all their stuff had been burned out, she had neither pencil nor paper nor envelope. Could she borrow?

She was invited in and set at the mean table, with tablet paper and pencil and a tattered envelope placed before her. She wrote to Britt, asking him to meet her the day after next. Then she borrowed another envelope, put Britt's sealed letter inside it, and in desperation addressed this to the postmaster at Bull Foot.

Talbot volunteered the information that he was going to Wagon Mound tomorrow, and Martha gave him the letter to mail.

Riding back home, she felt as if she were going to cry. *But, after all,* she reflected, *I don't know for sure.*

CHAPTER SIXTEEN

Martha wrote her letter on Sunday night. Talbot rode in with it Monday. It was delivered in Bull Foot that night, and the postmaster opened it early Tuesday morning. He saw it was simply an enclosure, but he did not open it. He had lived in Bull Foot long enough to know what happened to people who earned the displeasure of the Bannisters. Instead, he sent a rider out to the Dollar spread with the letter, a note with it explaining how he had come by it.

So Britt had the letter early Tuesday morning. He read it, savagely tore it to shreds, and went out to the corrals. He did not want to ride; he wanted to think. The fact that a daughter of Buck Tolleston had ordered him to see her filled him with fury. If he could hurt her right now, he would be glad to. Even the thought that he had talked to her, been with her, offered to marry her, made him angry. A Bannister crawling in front of a Tolleston. He wished savagely that he could avenge all these humiliations, and avenge them in some way that would agonize her. Always in his mind was the picture of that mother he hardly remembered, who had been killed—starved and overworked and beaten—by Buck Tolleston.

And thinking that, Britt had an idea. It was so sudden, so startling, that for a moment he was afraid to think of it. But the more he thought, the more he liked it. Everything was in his hands with which to do it.

He strode over to his father's office. Bannister was out, but Britt knew where the keys to the jail were. He got them, went over to the blacksmith shop where he hung his guns on a peg. Then he asked Symonds to come with him. Crossing to the jail, Britt unlocked the door and told Symonds to lock him in.

Webb and the three Montana hardcases were lounging on their bunks, their breakfast dishes on the bench in the middle of the room. They gave him no greeting, and he expected none.

"Stay in your bunk, Cousins," Britt said. "You others come over here in the corner."

It was a long room, so he could talk in a low tone to the three and not be heard by Webb. Webb didn't care anyway; he had ached and throbbed with the wound. The three Montana men squatted around Britt and he sat in the corner.

"I've got a job for you," he told them without preliminaries. "I want a man killed. Could you do it?"

"Not while we're in jail," Perry Warren said wryly.

"You'll be out."

"How much is in it?" Perry asked.

"Five hundred apiece."

Warren looked at the other two. "Suits me. But do we come back to this place when we're finished?"

"No. You got the old man mad the other night. I can get him over it quick enough. You'll be free today. You'll likely have other jobs to do, but I want this one done first."

Warren grinned crookedly and rubbed his beard-stubbled chin.

"O. K. What is it?"

"Ever hear of Buck Tolleston?"

They looked at each other and said they had. Britt told them more about him and who he was—the bank owner in Wagon Mound, a rancher, an enemy of all Bannisters. He finished with: "I want him shot. I don't care how you do it, only I want it done."

"Sounds easy to me," Warren said at last.

"It's not. It's in San Patricio. If you're caught, you'll face a hang-noose as sure as the sun'll rise tomorrow. I don't want you to get the idea it'll be easy. You may have to wait. You can't be seen, you can't ask questions. You'll just have to get his description from me, the description of the ranch, and wait for him. It may take a couple of days."

"It still sounds easy."

"Good," Britt said. "I'll have you out by tonight."

He called out the window for the blacksmith to unlock the door and went out. Webb, lying on his bunk, had not heard a word of it. He pretended he was napping. Presently, when the inevitable poker game started, he got up to join it. Since he had been in here, he had become friends wtih these men. They had yarned about themselves, and Webb had joined in, telling enough lies about himself to convince them he was outside the law like themselves. Too, they had respected him for not squealing on them to Bannister. He was one of them.

He got up, rolled a cigarette, and said, "What's goin' on in the outside world?"

"Good news," Warren said. "We're out of the jug tonight."

Webb lifted an eyebrow. "How come? Did you come clean to the old man?"

"Huh-uh. A job for young Bannister."

Webb pretended indifference. And then it came out. Britt Bannister wanted a man out of the way. Who was he? A gent by the name of Tolleston. Webb heard this calmly, no expression on his face except one of studied indifference. He had been about to ask if the pardon included him too, but now he knew it didn't. He had hit Britt Bannister in defense of a Tolleston, and Britt would hardly excuse that. Moreover, Webb had a hunch that this was being planned without Wake Bannister's knowledge. For if Wake Bannister wanted Buck Tolleston dead, he could have killed him any time these past fifteen years. Webb yawned.

"I'd take a job like that if it meant gettin' out of here."

The poker game grew tiresome, and Webb dropped out. He walked unsteadily over to the window facing the blacksmith shop and watched old Symonds at work. Yesterday, standing here, Webb had heard something queer. He had heard a man called Mitch say something to Bannister, and for the life of him he could not remember if he had heard the name before, but he was sure he had heard the voice. It sounded very familiar. Today he intended waiting here to see if he could hear the name again. It was tantalizing, not being able to remember.

It was close to noon when he heard men at Bannister's door. One voice he could identify as Hugo Meeker's, another as Bannister's. He listened and he could pick up the sound of Bannister's low, penetrating voice.

"He should be here about three, Hugo. I want Mitch to hear it, so bring him along."

"You sure you want him to?" Hugo said.

There was a pause. "Yes, I'm sure. He'll be reassured more by that than anything I can do."

Hugo said dryly, "I should think so." The door shut and Webb heard Hugo walk off. Webb stayed in the window, watching Symonds, wondering what was being planned. Sometime, somewhere, not here at Bannister's, he had heard this Mitch talk. If he could see his face, he might know him. But this barred window was in the same wall as the door to Bannister's office, and they were many feet apart. Unless a man walked over to Symonds's shop, it would be impossible to see him from this window.

Webb scowled and rubbed his chin thoughtfully. He could feel a several days' growth of red stubble over the hard line of his jaw. Suddenly his hand paused, and then he smiled slowly. He thought he had an idea.

Going back to the poker game, he sat down and took a hand. He kept scratching his face irritably, and when Warren noticed him, Webb said, "I'd give money to get this brush off my face."

"Why don't you shave?" Warren asked.

"No razor."

"I got one."

"No water. No mirror."

Warren grinned. "Hell, you ain't growed up unless you can shave without a mirror."

"I can't, though," Webb said.

"We'll get one," Warren told him. That noon, when their food was brought to them by the bull cook, Warren told him they wanted water and a mirror, and to see Britt Bannister if it was all right. In a short while, he returned with both. The others now decided to shave, and Webb let them take their turn.

When his turn came, he shaved. As he was washing his face, he managed to knock the mirror off the window sill and shatter it.

"That's a swell way to celebrate gettin' out of jail," Warren gibed.

Webb cursed mildly and dried his face, then stooped to pick up the pieces of the broken mirror. The largest he tucked inside his shirt, throwing the rest out of the window.

When the poker grew tiresome again, the game split up, and Warren and Manny ambled over to their bunks for a nap. Les, the third man, played solitaire, his back to the window. Webb drifted over to the barred window to watch Symonds. But once he was sure the others were not watching him, he propped the large shard of mirror outside the window, adjusting it so that it would reflect the face of the whole wing of the house. And then he waited, not knowing what time it was.

Soon he saw Hugo approach the office in company with another man who dressed and looked like Hugo himself. Lean, almost slouching, a half head taller than Hugo, he appeared to be a prosperous cattleman. He wore a white shirt, and his boots were black, hand-tooled, and expensive-looking. Only one gun, and that a pearl-handled one, was belted to his hips. Hugo ushered him into the office, and Webb waited. In a few seconds Hugo came out again and disappeared down the way between the outbuildings and the wing. Presently he returned with a companion.

This'll be Mitch, Webb thought, seeing them far down the way.

He studied the reflection in the mirror, watching Mitch, waiting until he got closer. And then, as Hugo and Mitch were about to step into the office, Webb got a good look at Mitch, and immediately he recognized him. That was Budrow, the man Tolleston had sent down to spy for him in Bull Foot! The man who had rawhided him that first night at the Broken Arrow.

For a moment Webb was amazed, and then the import of this knowledge came to him. Mitch—Budrow he'd heard Tolleston call him—had sold out Tolleston to Bannister!

It was this man who was responsible for the burning of Tolleston's and the other ranches. He had plotted with Bannister to raid San Patricio when Tolleston had all the outfits raiding Bull Foot.

Slowly Webb turned away from the window and sat down on the bench beneath it. No wonder San Patricio was defeated, with a Bannister spy in their camp.

What was this Mitch Budrow doing in there now? Who was the stranger? The latter could be any of the Wintering County ranchers, since Webb did not know them, but whoever he was, he shared in a new plan being hatched. And what that was Webb could not guess, but he was willing to bet that it concerned San Patricio County and Tolleston.

Webb rose and paced the floor, oblivious to the others in the room. Warren's voice yanked him out of his reverie.

"What in hell's got into you, fella? You're trampin' that floor until a man can't sleep."

Webb looked up at him, his eyes hard, a hot retort on his tongue. And then he smiled and sat down again. "Nothin'. I'm fed up with this bird cage."

"You'll be a damn sight more fed up," Warren said, and turned over in his bunk.

And Webb silently agreed with him, feeling a rage which only the knowledge of utter impotence can bring.

CHAPTER SEVENTEEN

WHEN HUGO came in the office with Mitch, Bannister indicated the stranger.

"Mitch, this is Clay Bogardus, from Texas. Mitch Budrow."

Mitch shook hands with the stranger, and they all took seats. Bogardus had an easy manner about him, but behind the chill blue of his eyes was a shrewdness that made Mitch uneasy. The man had a rather pleasant face, typical in its high cheekbones, its sun-bleached eyebrows, and in its absence of any expression except keen observance. Bogardus looked to Mitch like a prosperous cattleman, but one who still rode with his riders.

Bannister passed cigars all around, and the room was suddenly full of pleasant blue smoke.

"You know of this feud I've had with Tolleston and the San Patricio outfits, of course," Bannister said, by way of beginning.

Bogardus nodded. "Through Hugo."

"Yes. Then you know why I've called you."

"Not exactly," Bogardus said.

Bannister said, "It's not much. Those ranchers over there are strapped. They want to sell out. I've brought you up here to buy out the ranch of one of them."

"Who?"

"Lou Hasker—the Chain Link."

"How will I know him?" Bogardus asked.

Bannister thought a moment. "Redheaded, about twenty-six, medium big. You won't have any trouble meetin' him because Wardecker—he's the sheriff—will likely take you out."

Bogardus asked other questions, as to price, the date Bannister wanted the place, whether Bannister wanted to wait for a beef count, and other things. Bogardus was all business, and Mitch listened to the talk with a growing sense of curiosity. He wondered why Bannister wanted the Chain Link and what he would do with it when he got it, and why he was going about buying it in all this secrecy.

When the questions and answers were finished, Bannister said only, "I want the deed to the place inside a week. Get it for me."

He volunteered no other information to Bogardus, and Bogardus seemed to want none. Bogardus rose, shook hands all around, and left, with the parting admonition from Bannister that he was to catch the train at a water tank south of town and ride in like any other passenger.

Once Hugo and Bogardus were gone, Bannister said to Mitch, "Do you think Bogardus is a man to be trusted, Mitch?"

Mitch, flattered, thought a moment and said, "I'd say so. I reckon you made a good choice of men."

"I think so, too," Bannister said, evidently pleased. He turned to his desk. "Wait till Hugo comes back, Mitch. I'm goin' to tell you how I aim to work this whole thing out."

Hugo returned in a few minutes, and Bannister waved him to a seat and addressed himself to Mitch. "Have you wondered what's behind all this, Mitch? Have you decided I'm just an ordinary land hog?"

Mitch grinned. "I've wondered plenty."

Bannister smiled at him in a friendly way. "There's been a lot of things I've kept to myself, Mitch. The main

one is that the railroad is building through to Wagon
Mound. Next month some time their agents come in to
buy right of way through San Patricio."

The surprise on Mitch's face was obvious, but he was
politely silent.

"If that went through, Mitch, it would mean that San
Patricio County would boom. They'd ship stuff from
Wagon Mound without the loss of a head, and we
couldn't do anything to stop them."

"I see that."

"So I had to get in ahead of the railroad. I wanted to
bring this to a head while I still had time. That explains
the raid on San Patricio." Bannister regarded him closely.
"But the purchase of the Chain Link is another story."

"Why the Chain Link?" Mitch asked, gathering a courage of sorts.

"Ever ridden over the Chain Link range, Mitch?"

"Some of it."

"Ever noticed anything peculiar about it?"

Mitch scowled, and finally shook his head. "It's good
range. That's all I noticed."

Bannister looked over at Hugo and smiled a little, then
addressed Mitch again. "Ever noticed that Copperstone
Creek feeds most of the big ranches in San Patricio
County? Ever noticed that the Chain Link is the highest
range on the creek?"

"Come to think of it, it is," Mitch said.

"All right, ever noticed that when the Copperstone
comes out of the Chain Link Basin into the big canyon
it turns north?"

Again Mitch nodded.

Bannister leaned back in his chair and smiled faintly.
"A couple hundred dollars' worth of dynamite would
cave in those canyon walls to make a dam. It would back
the Copperstone up into the Basin. It would take less than
eight feet of water at the dam to shove the Copperstone

down a draw to the south and into Roan Creek. Roan Creek doesn't touch a single San Patricio ranch."

For a moment Mitch stared at him, and then comprehension showed on his face.

"And that," Bannister said, "is why I want the Chain Link. Bogardus will get a clear title to it. He'll turn it over to me. I'll move in with a strong crew. Before the railroad builds in there, I'll have every drop of water on the western slope of the Frying Pans running down the Copperstone. Those ranchers—including Buck Tolleston —will see a market set right down at their front door and they won't have a handful of cattle to ship, because they won't have the water to run them."

Mitch nodded in mute awe.

"And once I swing that, Mitch, I think I'll have a permanent place for you," Bannister concluded.

When Mitch had gone, Hugo sat down and cocked his feet up on the desk. The cigarette between his lips had died, and he was staring curiously at Bannister.

"I don't savvy it, Wake. That rat could peddle that to Hasker or Wardecker or Tolleston for half what they own."

"He won't," Bannister said. "This is the greatest favor anyone has ever done him. He's so damn grateful, he'd die for me now."

"I hope you're right. But I aim to keep a watch on him till tomorrow."

"Go ahead."

Hugo shook his head. "We shouldn't have waited this long."

Bannister didn't answer him for a moment. He was staring out the window, his keen and predatory face in repose. Presently he sighed. "Perhaps not. But I haven't got a taste for having a man killed while he sleeps. Nor one for killing him on the place where I live." And he added, "Not killing him that way, anyhow."

"Sure," Hugo said. He lighted his cigarette now. "You goin' to talk to them Montana men or am I?"

"I'll talk to them. Send them in. And after supper tonight, send Mitch in for his orders."

"His last," Hugo said grimly.

CHAPTER EIGHTEEN

H UGO OPENED the jail door. "The boss wants to see you," he said, from around his cigarette. All of them got up, including Webb.

Hugo said, "Not you, Red. Go back to sleep."

Webb lay back in his bunk and rolled a smoke as the others filed out and the door was shut. If he had had any doubts as to Bannister planning some new sort of trouble, he was sure of it now.

Warren and the others were gone half an hour. When they returned, they were smiling. Hugo locked them in again.

Webb looked at them curiously, scowling. "Goin' to another party, boys?"

"Sure," Warren said.

Webb cursed mildly. "I dunno what's the matter with me that I ain't asked to these things. Don't I take enough baths?"

"Even a shave didn't help you none," Warren said good-naturedly, his crooked grin wolfish and amused. He sat down at the table and pulled out a handful of gold coins, which he proceeded to count into three equal piles. He took one, Les and Manny the remaining two. Then Warren tipped his chair back against the wall and looked at Webb. Webb knew he was in for a rawhiding, and he covered up his impatience to know what this was all about by thumbing his nose at Warren.

"Hell, you're just sore," Warren said.

"Sure. Who wouldn't be?"

Warren winked at one of his companions. "You always got to remember two things, fella. Never go anywhere you ain't asked. Never do anything you ain't paid for."

"A swell chance I had of bein' asked here," Webb growled. "Even if I did want to work for Bannister, he wouldn't have me."

"Maybe you got a weak stomach," Warren suggested.

Webb looked up at him. "It ain't showed up yet if I have."

"Could you shoot a man in the back for money?" Warren drawled.

"Easy, Perry," Les warned. "You recollect what the old man said."

"Hell with him," Warren said arrogantly. "We got half our money. He can't keep a thing like this quiet, anyway."

"All right. I'm just tellin' you," Les said, earnestly, his game of solitaire interrupted.

Dan Warren said, "The thing I can't figure out is this: How does Bannister stand to make any money by having a thirty-a-month puncher killed. Is it worth what he's paying us?"

Webb's pulse quickened, but he allowed only an expression of faint curiosity to show on his face. He glanced over at Les and said, "He's talking to you, Les. I don't know what this is all about."

"He's talking too much," Les said grimly.

"But what does this puncher know?" Warren insisted. "He don't even work around here."

"A stranger?" Webb asked idly.

"Seems so. Leastways, Bannister said he was givin' us the same instructions to get to Ted Bannister's as he was givin' this fella he wants shot. Sounds like he didn't know the country as good as us."

Les slammed down his cards. "There you go, Perry, shootin' off your mouth!"

"What about?" Perry asked innocently.

"Tellin' him where this job is goin' to be pulled off!"

"What if I did?" Warren said, with rising temper. "Who the hell is he? He's in jail. Who could he tell?"

"That's all right," Webb cut in soothingly. "I don't give a damn about knowin'. I'm not askin' you to tell me."

"Go ahead and ask," Warren said sharply, glaring at Les. "It'll take more'n an old woman to make me keep my mouth shut."

Les growled. "Old woman or not, keep your mouth shut, Perry."

Warren slowly rose out of his chair and stalked stiff-legged over to the card table. "And who's goin' to make me?" he asked gently. "You, Les? Or Manny?"

"Leave me out of this," Manny said from his bunk. "I don't care if you put it to music."

Warren glared at Les. "Well?"

Les put both hands on the table and rose, facing Warren. "All right," he said thickly. "I am! I got a third stake in this job and I'll get it, if anything goes—"

He never finished. Warren struck out viciously, his thudding fist catching Les square in the mouth. The blow sent Les against the chair, which tripped him and sent him sprawling on his back. Warren walked over to him and watched him drag himself to his feet and shake his head to clear it.

"Go ahead," Warren taunted.

Les shook his head. "Forget it," he said. It was obvious to Webb that Warren was the master here. Warren thought so, too, and wanted to prove it, and to prove that he was stepping into the place vacated by Lute.

Les went over to the table and sat down. Warren followed him and went around to the other side of the table and leaned both hands on it, his ugly face close to Les.

"Listen to this, Cousins," Warren said slowly, looking at Les. "I think the name of the man we're goin' to shoot is Budrow, Mitch Budrow, if I recollect right. We're goin' to get turned out of here tonight and cache ourselves on the road to the Spade B, over east. This Budrow is comin' along sometime early tomorrow mornin'. I don't know why we're goin' to kill him. If I did, I'd tell you. We're gettin' three hundred apiece for it. Anything else you want to know?" He was watching Les, trying to rawhide him into making a play.

Webb drawled, "I never even wanted to know that."

"O. K., Perry," Les said, shrugging. "You'll get it along with the rest of us."

"Get what?" Warren said truculently.

Manny, from his bunk, said, "Lay off, Perry. Hell, you got no row, now."

Warren straightened up. "I just wanted to let you two tinhorns know who's callin' the turn here."

Les shrugged and went back to his solitaire. Warren grinned at Webb and they relaxed.

Back in his bunk, Webb turned over in his mind what he had goaded Warren into admitting. At last he was sure of the part Mitch Budrow had played in this war. A traitor, and one who was getting his just deserts. And once Mitch was out of the way, only Hugo and Wake Bannister would know the whole story of how San Patricio had been defeated.

Webb thought of the conference earlier in the afternoon, a conference attended by a stranger, Mitch, Hugo, and Bannister. Had they been plotting further trouble, another raid, perhaps, that would win all of San Patricio and its range for Bannister? Mitch Budrow would know, for he held the key to all the strange things that had happened here. And tomorrow morning, because he knew so much, Bannister was going to put him out of the way.

Silently Webb cursed. If he were free, he might be able to prevent this killing, and to capture Mitch and take him back to Tolleston. Mitch might even be persuaded to talk if he knew that Bannister intended killing him. But Webb was not free. He was in jail, with enough knowledge in his mind to blow up this feud, but still helpless, worse than useless.

He stared at the ceiling, disgusted with himself. Reluctantly he forced himself to talk now, because he did not want it to appear that he gave any value to what he had just learned.

He said to Warren, "What's goin' to happen with this other job of yours, young Britt's?"

"He can go to hell," Warren said shortly. "We're not workin' for him."

Les looked up. "I'll take that job, Perry. You and Manny take the other."

"You will like hell," Warren said curtly. "You'll do what I tell you. If we tag Tolleston, we'll have old man Bannister and all of San Patricio County on our necks. We'd have to jump the country. Now we got an easy job, and we'll likely get more, accordin' to what Bannister said. Huh-uh. I take orders from the old man, as long as the work keeps comin'. And you'll take orders from me."

Les only glared at him. Manny didn't seem interested.

Webb moved restlessly. "I wish you could swing that job over to me, but I don't reckon young Bannister would do it."

"Why not?"

"I hit him the other day over what he said about Tolleston's girl."

Warren asked curiously, "You like her?"

Webb made a wry face. "No. I just like her better than I do young Bannister."

Warren chuckled. "That's no way to make money."

"I know that," Webb said sourly. "I wish I'd had sense enough to keep my head. Maybe I'd 'a' been out of here, then."

"I'll talk to young Bannister tonight and see what he thinks about it," Warren told him.

Webb let it ride that way. At supper time they all ate together, and afterward Warren and his companions were freed by Hugo. Webb was left alone in the jail.

Webb couldn't be sure that Warren would keep his word and talk with Britt; it was a thin chance and there was no reason why Britt should bother with it. On the other hand, he just might, and Webb had to be prepared for a possible visit. There was nothing he wanted to discuss with Britt. All he wanted was to get close enough to him to get his gun.

Webb hunted the room over carefully for something he could use for a weapon. He found nothing. Every bit of loose metal had been removed. If he ripped the leg off a chair, it would be too bulky a weapon to hide.

And thinking this, he had an idea. He walked over to a chair and turned it upside down. Then he looked around the room. The only other articles of furniture were a heavy table, the stand holding the water bucket, a big bench, a smaller bench, and a rickety chair.

Webb set to work. He twisted the legs off the chair, pulling the wood away from the nails. Then he flattened the nails out and, after a difficult five minutes of balancing, had the chair so it would stand on its legs. He placed it near the table in a position where Britt would be unlikely to move it when he sat down. He did the same with the big bench. After fifteen minutes patient work he had all the seats, with the exception of the small bench, torn to pieces and reconstructed so that, while they looked natural enough, anyone trying to sit on them would be thrown to the floor.

Webb took the small bench, pulled it up to the table,

and laid out a game of solitaire. Hoping this would relieve the monotony of waiting, he played through several hands, but even a run-out did not serve to distract him. The minutes dragged, and he grew increasingly skeptical. Britt Bannister would probably laugh when Warren told him of Webb's offer. Perhaps Warren would even forget it.

He had almost resigned himself to Bannister's not coming when he heard footsteps outside approaching the door. He dealt out a spread of solitaire and waited, cards in hand, as he heard the door being unlocked and unbolted.

Britt Bannister stood in the doorway.

"Howdy," Webb said.

Bannister closed the door and leaned against it. Webb noticed he was wearing a gun. Although he was dressed in a gaudy blue shirt and yellow neckerchief, pearl-gray Stetson, and whipcord trousers, there was a look about Bannister's face that belied his air of ease and elegance. A scowl creased his forehead and he looked tired, weary, and a bit suspicious.

"Did you think I'd fall for that offer you made, Warren?" he asked surlily.

Webb just looked at him and did not get up. He went back to his cards. "You're here, ain't you?"

"To tell you you'll damn well stay in here for another week. And when you get out of here, it'll be to step into the Wintering County jail."

Webb smiled thinly. "And from there to the pen at Yuma, if you can swing it. Is that it?"

"That's it."

"The hell it is," Webb drawled. "I don't reckon so."

"No? You'll see. Maybe you'd 'a' been better off if you'd minded your business and not snooped around to find out what I was talkin' to Warren about."

"Shut it," Webb said indolently, playing his hand of

solitaire. "You can't keep four men locked in a room for days and not expect them to talk."

"You won't get the chance again," Britt said quickly. He put his hand on the door bolt.

"That all you come to tell me?" Webb asked mildly.

"That'll be plenty."

"But that ain't why I sent for you," Webb went on casually. "I aim to buy my way out of here."

"You couldn't steal enough money to do it," Britt said.

"Not with money. I hadn't even thought of that."

Britt paused, saying nothing, waiting.

"What you aim to do," Webb drawled, "and what you don't want me or these other hardcases to know you aim to do, is to get even with Martha Tolleston, isn't it?"

Britt removed his hand from the door and walked slowly toward Webb. "Another crack like that and I don't think I'll even turn you over to the sheriff."

Webb shrugged. "All I'm tryin' to do is tell you without you cuttin' down on me that I know a way you can get even with her."

The expression on Britt's face did not change, except perhaps that it showed a little more suspicion and a little more curiosity. "How?" he asked.

Webb reached in his pocket and drew out a folded piece of paper which he held out to Britt. Britt walked across to the table and took it.

"First," Webb said, "that's a reasonably accurate map of the Broken Arrow buildin's, water holes, creeks and such, isn't it?"

Britt looked at it. "No."

Webb frowned. "No?"

"Certainly not. If you got this anywhere near scale, the Roan forks is a good three miles farther west. And I never saw a spring where this is marked. And I—"

"Wait," Webb said, fumbling in his pocket for a pencil. "That's important. Mark it down."

"What for?" Britt asked, but he reached for the pencil. He was interested as well as mystified, Webb could see.

"You'll find out. Mark it down."

Webb leaned down to mark the map. He was directly in the light of the overhead lamp, and his shadow made Webb's faint drawing almost invisible. Instinctively Britt glanced around and saw a chair to the side of him, quartering the table.

He sank into it, and at the same time Webb upended the table. Britt hit the chair and it fell away from him. He threw up his hand to pull at the table to catch himself. The table came over on top of him, and Webb in a dive right behind it.

Britt had already sensed the trap and his hand was clawing at his gun, but before he could wrap his fingers around the butt, he crashed down on his side, pinning his hand under him. And then Webb lighted on him, a hundred and seventy pounds of explosive fury.

Britt instinctively raised his arm to shield his face, and Webb drove a fist into his stomach. Gagging, Britt clinched with him, but Webb, spraddle-legged over him, was not to be tied up or thrown. He slugged again at Britt's belly and followed up by leaning in with crooked elbow. Britt's arm came down in a protective, automatic gesture. Webb, watching, seized his chance. As hard and quick as he could manage it, he drove a looping, knuckle-studded fist at Britt's temple. Twice, three times he slugged before he realized that his first blow had done the work. Like a deflated balloon, Britt relaxed under him.

Grinning, Webb rose and ripped the handkerchief from Britt's neck. He gagged him, then with strips torn from the blanket on the bunk securely trussed his hands and feet and then hog-tied him. It was the work of only a few more moments for Webb to strap on the shell belt and gun, and to lift Britt into the bunk and turn his face to the wall. Then he righted the table, spread the cards out on it, picked up the chair and threw the pieces in one of the bunks, and surveyed the room. To the casual beholder it would appear that Webb was asleep in his bunk, having left the light on.

At the door Webb paused and listened. No sound. He melted out the door into the welcome darkness, shutting and padlocking the door, and headed for the corrals. Boldly he walked into the saddle shed and by the light of a match found a good-looking saddle. Slinging it over his shoulder, he headed for the small corral behind the larger one. This was the corral where Bannister and Britt kept their ponies wanted for immediate use. It was not far from Gonzales's quarters in the barn, but Webb went boldly ahead. There was a light in the barn, too.

Webb singled out the horse that seemed the most gentle and saddled it. Midway through the task, he heard Gonzales call, "That you, Britt?"

"Hell with you, fella," Webb said carelessly, and he saw the door shut. Gonzales, used to being addressed in this way by Britt, had withdrawn from the door.

Webb rode slowly out of the settlement toward the south, where there were no houses. Once free of the place, he headed southeast for Bull Foot. He had a horse and a gun and his freedom. All he needed now was a little information.

CHAPTER NINETEEN

MITCH BUDROW was whistling. If he had stopped to realize it, he would have known that it was the first time he had done such a thing in two years. But now he was happy. Things were different. He was a valued man of Wake Bannister's, and that meant protection against all law for years to come. Whenever Mitch had doubts about Bannister valuing him, all he had to do was think of what Wake Bannister had disclosed to him yesterday. Mitch was proud of that. Of course, he had done Bannister a great favor in telling him the details of the Bull Foot raid, but that was just a plain case of listening and reporting. No, it wasn't that. Bannister had seen his loyalty, had seen that he used his head, and Bannister was a man who rewarded those faithful to him. Mitch's reward was the sharing of this momentous secret. Why, even Ted Bannister over at the Spade B, where he was going this morning, hadn't been told all of Wake's plans. That's why Mitch was going to see him.

So Mitch whistled. It was a bright morning, with a ground breeze that would not die yet for an hour. Mitch looked at the country and found much to admire. He had left the Dollar just before dawn. Ahead of him, its grass ruffled by the slow wind, the land tilted up to a pair of buttes in the distance. He had followed the draw east of the Dollar, which Wake had told him would put him on the stage road to Wagon Mound. He was to follow this to the first road that forked to the left. This was the road to Ted Bannister's Spade B.

Mitch didn't have any trouble finding the road. He was riding along without a care in the world, a little of the old impudence back in his eyes.

When he saw a rider ahead of him coming his way, he made no move to pull off into the brush, although that was his impulse and he found himself wanting to. Why should he? He was a Dollar hand, as good a man as he would meet. Better, probably.

Mitch didn't notice the cowboy very carefully. He was walking his horse, and he had his head down, and Mitch could hear him whistling.

When Mitch was close enough to him, he called, "Howdy, friend."

The man looked up quickly, and in the same motion a gun appeared in his right hand, and its barrel looked as big as a cave to Mitch.

Mitch dragged his gaze from the gun to the man's face, and seeing it, Mitch's happiness died. He licked his lips.

"You, Cousins," he said faintly.

Webb nodded. "Better unstrap your belt and hang it over the horn, Mitch, then get down and lead your horse off the road."

"This—this ain't a—"

"No," Webb said quietly. "I don't reckon so, although I may change my mind after I hear your story."

Mitch took off his gun belt and hung it over his saddle horn, then dismounted and wearily led his horse off the trail and down into a shallow arroyo. Webb followed and dismounted.

"Sit down, Mitch," Webb ordered. "This may take some time."

Mitch sat against the arroyo bank while Webb, holstering his gun, squatted against the other bank. Webb rolled a smoke and lighted it and then squinted at

Mitch, who was waiting patiently, his face harried and humble.

"I got out last night, Mitch. I rode into Bull Foot to ask a few questions." He regarded Mitch coldly. "Twenty-some riders ambushed, Mitch. Are you proud of it?"

Mitch cleared his throat. "I had to."

"Had to sell out the man you worked for. Sold his friends, and him, too, to the guns of a damn maniac."

"I had to," Mitch repeated. "I always worked for Bannister. If I hadn't, I'd be dead now."

Webb's eyes were cold with contempt. "Every ranch of any size in San Patricio is burned, Mitch. Wagon Mound is burned. Men are dead. Do you think your cheap carcass is worth that?"

Mitch said nothing.

"You work for Bannister, Mitch?"

"Yes."

"He likes you, trusts you?"

Mitch looked up. "Yes," he said cautiously.

"Did you know I was locked up with three of those Montana gunmen?"

"I heard it."

"Know where they are?"

Mitch shook his head.

"They're up this trail, waitin', cached behind boulders. They got three hundred dollars apiece in their pockets from Bannister. They're waitin' for someone, Mitch. Know who?"

Mitch shook his head dumbly.

"You."

Mitch licked his lips. The news settled on him like a blanket of grief. He didn't even doubt this redhead's word, because it all seemed true, seemed that this was what he should have expected all the time. All the other things, the trust that Bannister put in him, the confidence he professed in him, were artificial, and he might have known it. All Bannister wanted was to get him away from the ranch long enough to gun him. He said quietly, "Yes."

Surprised, Webb asked, "You expected it?"

"Yes. If I'd used my head, I might have." He stared down at the sand a long time, then he said calmly, "You one of 'em, too?"

"Not me," Webb said. "I'm turning you over to somebody else. Somebody that'll want to talk to you just as I did."

"Tolleston?"

"That's right."

Mitch shuddered. His eyes were filled with blank despair. "Not that, Cousins. If that's my ticket, I'd ruther you shot me now."

"Rather be shot than hung," Webb murmured.

Mitch nodded. He knew what his life would be worth over there. He knew what it would be worth here.

Webb said, "Well, come along, fella. That's where you're goin' anyway." He stood up, waiting for Mitch.

But Mitch did not stir. He only shook his head slowly. "No, I ain't. You better shoot me right now. I ain't goin' over to San Patricio."

Webb said, softly, "The hell you're not," and palmed up his gun.

Mitch scrambled to his feet, facing Webb. He was breathing hard, and his face was a dead white, his eyes wild with terror.

"Come ahead!" he said flatly. "Fight me or shoot me, I don't care which! But I ain't goin' to Tolleston unless I go dead. Come ahead!"

Webb hesitated before the genuine terror he saw. He felt the same kind of pity for Mitch that he felt for a cornered coyote, but, nevertheless, it was pity.

"Why, you damned fool," he drawled. "If you stay here, Bannister'll hunt you out and gun you like he would a rattlesnake. Over there you'll get justice and a trial, which is more than you deserve!"

"Go ahead and shoot," Mitch said doggedly. "Maybe I will get killed here. I know I will. But I'd rather do that than go back with you!"

Webb watched him, puzzled. His jaw muscles bulged a little and he hefted his gun. "I'm not goin' to fool with you, Budrow. If you're next to Bannister, you know what he's plannin'. Do you think I'm goin' to turn you loose, when I have a chance to find that out from you?" He took a step toward Mitch. "I'll tell you anything you want to know," Mitch said quietly, "but you ain't takin' me alive!"

Webb stopped. He said slowly, "All right, tell it."

And then, talking so fast that his words were almost a jumble, Mitch told Webb of Bannister's plans. It came out in a torrent of words, all of the details of the plan to buy the Chain Link, to divert the water before the railroad built in, and thereby crown the San Patricio defeat with this last sardonic thrust that would turn the county into a worthless desert. As Mitch talked, Webb knew he was telling the truth. The man was talking from sheer terror, and what he said about the railroad and about Hasker showed a knowledge he could have picked up only from Bannister. Every question Webb asked was answered.

Mitch was talking for his life. He told of how he first met Bannister, how he had spied on Tolleston, how he had transmitted the plans to Bannister, how he had seen the massacre, and how he knew then he was slated to die. All of it, his fear, these long days of panic, came out in pitiable sincerity, until Webb wanted to look away. He felt a shame for Mitch that made him want to shut the man's mouth and stop the crawling and pleading and cringing.

Mitch finished: "That's all I know. I've told you all.

I'm guilty of everything you say—but I ain't goin' back to San Patricio. I'm scared of Bannister, but I'm more scared of them. If you want to shoot, go ahead."

Webb cuffed his Stetson back and looked meditatively at Mitch. "If I don't take you, what'll you do?"

"I don't know," Mitch said miserably.

"Run back to Bannister and tell him you've tipped his hand for him?"

Mitch looked up quickly. "God, no!" he whispered. "He'd kill me before I'd finished! He'd do worse! He'd torture me. I don't know how, but I know he would." The shudder that moved his body was real, genuine fear.

Webb weighed the truth of this. Mitch could gain nothing from Bannister by returning to him now—nothing except a horrible death. He was marked to die anyway, because he knew so much. That was inevitable. And if he returned to Bannister with the confession that he had told Bannister's plans, then Bannister's rage would be boundless. No, Mitch wasn't apt to return to Bannister.

And what about taking him to Tolleston? Webb could almost see the fury of that little man when he heard Mitch's story. And once it got around the county, there would be no trial. These men loved justice, but there was a limit to that love. They would yank Mitch out of the jail and lynch him. While he probably deserved it, Webb couldn't bring a man back to that. It would be on his conscience forever. And he couldn't stand here and level a gun and shoot him.

"I won't take you to Tolleston, Budrow," Webb said slowly, watching Mitch. "I won't take you anywhere. Bannister's reward poster will take care of you. If you're smart, you'll light out of this country on a high lonesome and keep ridin' till you've ridden a *remuda* to death. And then ride after that. You may live a year, but I doubt it. Me, I hope you don't."

He turned to his horse and rode off. Mitch did not even look up to watch him go. But he heard him, and the words Webb had spoken were graven in Mitch's memory.

Mitch was thinking clearer and straighter than he had ever thought in his life. If he returned to the Dollar with the news that he had given the plot away, he would be killed before he finished telling. If he returned and said nothing about meeting Webb, he would be killed anyway. If he rode out of this country, then he would be the prey of any man with a memory for faces. Weren't there already reward posters out? And wasn't Cousins right when he said that Bannister would raise the reward ante until it totaled a sum that would induce men to leave home and jobs to hunt him out? He couldn't stay in Wintering County. He couldn't hide in San Patricio. He couldn't ride away from both.

For many long minutes Mitch sat there, sifting sand through his fingers, thinking. Finally he looked up at the sky, and the expression on his face was one of surprise. He looked around him, as if all this was unfamiliar. He looked at his horse, standing hipshot in the warm sunlight, stomping an occasional fly. The jingling of the bridle chain attracted him. Funny, he thought, how you noticed little things like that, or the markings on your horse at a time like this. For instance, he had not noticed this morning that the horse he had snaked out of the corral had a perfect star on his forehead. Mitch noticed a lot of things like that, trivial things, and all the while he had a sense of inexorable time passing.

Presently he got up and walked over to his horse. The gun slung in its belt over the saddle horn attracted him. He took out the .45 and looked at its sheen. He cocked it and then looked down the barrel. It looked big. He shuddered and let it off cock and then threw it away. The belt he threw away, too.

Then he mounted and sought the road. He didn't

pause there but resolutely turned his horse toward the Twin Buttes.

He was glad Cousins hadn't told him where those three Montana hardcases were forted up. He hoped they were good shots.

Presently he started thinking about his mother back in Texas. Would Wake send her money as a sop to his conscience? Perhaps. It didn't matter much, because he had sent her enough as it was. He had never told her about Mitch killing that girl in Tucson because, after all, Bannister was a gentleman in some ways. That would be one of the ways.

Mitch was thinking about that girl when the shots came.

Warren, Les, and Manny were good shots. They did not need to be, however, for they were not more than twelve feet from where Mitch passed.

The shots drove Mitch over the saddle horn onto his horse's neck. The horse shied, sloping Mitch off, and then stampeded.

He lay there dead in the sand, three neat holes in his back, while the sound of shells being ejected from guns clicked out in that sunny morning silence.

"Now we can smoke," Warren said.

CHAPTER TWENTY

W<small>EBB</small> did not make the mistake of thinking he could ride into Tolleston's place and be welcomed. He knew Buck still thought him one of the original bank robbers, hired by Bannister, and his belief had been vindicated by Webb's presence at the burning of the Broken Arrow.

First, Buck would have to be made to listen to reason. Webb was prepared to put up with the insults and the abuse, possibly attempted shooting, that was sure to come from Tolleston. He only hoped that Martha Tolleston, with the charity natural to a woman, would prevent Buck from doing anything rash until he had heard Webb's story.

Webb rode all day, avoiding trails and roads, but holding to a course which would inevitably bring him to the Broken Arrow. When darkness fell, he was on reasonably familiar ground, and he proceeded north.

His first glimpse of the Broken Arrow was from the same place he had seen it last with Lute and Shorty. There was a camp of sorts out under the trees, and by the light of the big fire Webb could see the shell of the house.

Dismounting, he tied his horse to a cedar and slung his gun belt over the saddle horn. He hated this, but it was better to put all temptation aside. He might lose his temper, and once he went for a gun, there would be no quitting until he or Tolleston was down.

He made his way down the slope, and as he approached the fire he could distinguish people. Martha was sitting by her dad, who was seated on a chuck box. Charley was cleaning up after supper, with the aid of Mrs. Partridge. The hands were sprawled out around the fire, listening to Buck.

Webb walked on slowly, careful to make no noise. He chose to approach the fire in full view of Buck, should he look up.

It was one of the hands, Chuck Martin, who first caught sight of the man approaching the fire. Martin straightened up, his hand falling to his gun.

Buck saw that gesture and looked up, just as Webb stepped into the circle of firelight. For a moment no one moved, and then Buck exploded off the chuck box, his hand streaking for his gun.

And as Webb had hoped, Martha intervened. She seized her father's wrist. "Dad, dad, don't! Don't you see he hasn't a gun!"

Buck started to brush her roughly aside, when Martin rose, gun in hand. Webb didn't move, didn't attempt to run or to dodge. There was a faint smile on his lean, freckled face, a look of amused patience. Martin, cocking his gun, looked beyond Webb into the night.

"I'm alone," Webb said. "I came to talk."

"I got a gun on him, Buck," Martin said.

Tolleston strode around the fire, Martha behind him. Stopping before Webb, Tolleston said ominously, "You didn't come back here to hang, Cousins. What's behind this?"

Webb said, "I want to talk." He looked at Martha for help, but her face was tense. She, too, suspected this was a trap.

Buck pointed his gun at Webb and said, without turning, "Chuck, take a *pasear* up over that ridge. Ed, go out and listen for riders across the creek. Charley, douse that fire."

"Slow down," Webb said easily. "You'll only have to build it up again. I escaped from Bannister's this mornin'. I got a stolen horse and a gun belt on the saddle over on the ridge. I ain't been followed. I'm alone."

Martha said, "I think he means it, dad. Don't be so excited."

"Get away from that fire, all of you!" Buck ordered sharply. "I'm going to see. Get on, Charley."

They waited in the half-gloom of the trees until Ed returned, and a little later, Charley.

"His horse is there," Charley said.

"I don't hear a thing, Buck," Ed said.

Tolleston seemed to hesitate. Then one of the hands who had vanished off in another direction returned. Webb was surprised to see that it was Stoop, the long cowboy he had fought with the first night, and whom Tolleston had sent across the desert to check upon Webb's past.

Webb smiled at seeing him, but did not speak.

Tolleston said, "Stay out there, Regan. You, Charley, go up on the ridge and keep a lookout. If anything looks funny or you hear anything, shoot once." Then he turned to Webb. "Get over here," he said, indicating the fire.

Webb was prodded over to the chuck box, and Martin searched him for hide-outs after which Tolleston ordered him to sit down. Tolleston never holstered his gun, and his eyes were dancing with anger.

"So you've come crawlin' back here, hopin' you can lie yourself out of a hang-noose? Well, go ahead and talk, son. Talk me deaf, if you can."

"Can I smoke?" Webb asked.

Tolleston nodded. Webb was stalling for time, hoping Tolleston would cool off. His fingers were steady as he built a smoke and lighted it. A way to begin would be the hardest.

He looked up at Buck and Martha. "Sit down, all of you. I reckon this'll take most of the evenin'."

"What will?" Buck snarled.

"The story of how Bannister is finally goin' to drive you men to the wall—and if he does, you'll stay there this time." When Buck did not move, Webb said again, "Sit down. I won't run. And this'll take time."

Tolleston dragged a saddle out and told Martha to sit on it. Then Buck kicked the fire and ordered Chuck and Ed to get rifles and sit across the fire. For himself he dragged a spring seat from the wagon into the firelight and sat by Martha. He held a six-gun loosely in his hand.

"All right," he said curtly. "I want to see you beg. Go ahead. Make me a deal, you cheap killer! Trade me what you've overheard for money."

"Dad!" Martha said softly.

"But to begin with," Buck said. "You offer me any kind of a deal at all, and I won't save you for a trial. You still want to talk?"

Webb smoked calmly, his face averted, watching the fire. When Buck had ceased talking, Webb looked at him. "You through?"

Buck started to rise, a strangled noise in his throat, but Martha held him down.

Webb said, "Mitch Budrow is the man who betrayed you, Tolleston. He's always been in Bannister's pay. A little over ten months ago he stumbled into a line camp up in the Fryin' Pans, didn't he?"

Martha said, "Yes."

"But he hadn't come over the mountains then. He'd been a week at Bannister's Dollar spread. Hugo Meeker found him starvin' to death at a dry water hole the other side of the mountains and brought him home. Mitch was runnin' from somethin'. I don't know what. But Bannister hit on the idea of sendin' him over to one of your line camps, hopin' you'd take him in. He was so weak Hugo had to pack him within a hundred yards of the shack. Your men took him in, didn't they?"

Tolleston glanced obliquely at Martha and then looked steadily at Webb.

"That's partly right," he said. "About finding Mitch. But Mitch was killed, fightin' for me. He was no traitor."

"Where is he?" Webb drawled.

"Dead. With plenty other good men!"

"I talked to him this mornin'," Webb said dryly. "He's been at the Dollar since the night of the raid. He's the man who sold you out. When you sent him down to see if those hardcases were in Bull Foot, he rode to Bannister and told him what you'd planned. Bannister set his trap—warned the storekeepers and townspeople in Bull Foot that the raid was comin'."

"That's a lie!" Buck said. "Mitch never left my side!"

"Is it?" Webb drawled. "All right. Mitch walked out of the cattleman's meeting and wrote a letter to the station agent in Bull Foot, enclosing a letter to Bannister. That letter told Bannister how many men to expect, what time they were comin', who would be ridin', and how they would do it."

Tolleston had his mouth open to reply in furious rebuttal when he thought of the afternoon of that meeting. Mitch had told him he was going to write a letter. Buck never saw the letter to confirm the address, but the fact remained, Mitch did write a letter. He only said, "Go on."

"One moment," Martha put in. "How do you know all this?"

"Mitch told me," Webb said calmly. "He told me a lot of things. Would you like to hear them?"

"If you say he's a traitor," Martha insisted hotly, "how would we know the truth of them? Why did he tell you? How did—"

"Do you want to hear them?" Webb cut in calmly. "I

don't know if they're true. But I know if they are true, then you and your dad won't have a penny to your name two months from now."

Buck said, "Get on with it. What lies did he tell you?"

"He told me this," Webb said. "The agents for the Southwestern Railroad will be in Wagon Mound in another month, buying right of way for the line they're going to extend to Wagon Mou—"

Buck Tolleston was out of his seat, and facing Webb. "You damn fool, do you know what you're sayin'?" he asked huskily.

Martha said rapidly, "How do you know? How do you know?"

Webb looked around him. All these men were on their feet, waiting for his answer. "I know from Mitch. Mitch knew from Bannister. The railroad has already written him about grading teams. They've named the date their agents are comin'."

"Why haven't they written us?" Buck whipped out.

"They did. Hugo Meeker stuck up the mail stage and got their letter to you."

Buck looked swiftly at Charley. That much, unbelievable as it was, rang true, for the stage had been held up, and the sacks strangely returned to it.

Chuck Martin said to Webb, "What good will that do Bannister, stealing the letter? It ain't goin' to keep the railroad out."

"Mitch told me why," Webb said quietly.

"Why?"

Webb talked straight at Tolleston. "Because Bannister wants time. He planned this raid on Wagon Mound and San Patricio to get these ranchers discouraged. He knew some of them would want to sell, but he knew they wouldn't sell if the railroad was comin' in."

"They'll find out sooner or later if it's true," Buck said swiftly. "What's time got to do about it?"

"Because he wants Lou Hasker's Chain Link," Webb said slowly. "He figures Hasker will sell. He—"

"Not to him," Martin said.

"No. To his buyer." Webb raised a hand. "Let me finish. Bannister has got these ranchers in the frame of mind he wants them. They're whipped. Some want to pull out. They don't know about the railroad, and he doesn't want them to. He's got one of his men on the way to Wagon Mound right now. That man is going to Buy Lou Hasker's Chain Link if he can get it. He is—"

"Why the Chain Link?" Buck cut in.

"Because where the Copperstone comes out of the Chain Link Basin into the canyon there's a natural place for a dam. He'll get it by dynamiting the cliff walls down. That'll back up the Copperstone until it takes off down a draw into Roan Creek. Once that's done, you men will whistle for water. And it doesn't matter then if the railroad is at your door. Without water you can't raise cattle to ship." He looked from Tolleston to Martin to Martha. "Does that make sense?"

"You said something about a buyer," Buck said. "What buyer?"

"Clay Bogardus is his name. He's backed by Bannister's money and the minute he gets the deed to the Chain Link, he'll turn it over to Bannister."

Buck stood utterly still, trying to absorb all this. Martin watched him, waiting for a sign of his belief.

Martha said softly, "Dad, do you hear? Do you know what it means?"

Buck turned away and walked over and sat down. Webb thought he knew what was running through Tolleston's mind. Buck was being asked to take the word of a man he thought a criminal.

"Why should I believe that?" Buck asked at long last. "I've never found that you told the truth in anything else you've ever said. I—"

"Stoop is back," Webb said quietly. "What did he have to report about my past?"

Buck flushed. "It was like you said—or every man in that country will gladly lie for you. But that don't change what you've turned into."

"I haven't changed, Tolleston. It's that damned suspicious mind of yours," Webb said sharply.

Buck half rose. "Suspicious?" he said, his voice hard in anger. "Explain it all, then! Why did you run out that first day I let you have a horse? Tell me that? Why did you run to Wintering?"

Webb's gaze shuttled to Martha, but she could not meet his look.

"I'm afraid that'll have to ride, Tolleston. Just a natural thing to do," Webb said carelessly.

"And you—"

Martha's voice cut through Buck's speech and stopped it dead, as she said, "Tell the truth."

Webb closed his mouth and looked away.

"Then I'll tell it," Martha said quietly. "He didn't run away, dad. He was taken away—taken over into Wintering County and kept prisoner at the Bannisters' place."

Buck turned swiftly to her. "How do you know?"

"Because I saw him taken, dad. I made the suggestion. The man that took him was—was Britt Bannister."

A flush of shame colored Martha's face, but she faced her father with head up. Before he could protest, she went on:

"Britt Bannister and I had been seeing each other for months, dad. That's where I went. We both hated this fight between our fathers and their friends. We laughed at it. Britt wanted to marry me. I wouldn't do that—on your account, dad. But we saw each other. When you sent Webb Cousins out to spy on us, he did. Only we discovered him. We were afraid if we let him go, he would go back and tell you about our meeting, so Britt took him over to their place."

Buck looked as if someone had hit him. He sank back on the seat and lowered his head on his chest. Martha put a hand on his shoulder.

"I'm sorry, dad. I didn't want to sneak, but I wanted even less to hurt you. And it was my life, and Britt's was his own! We had to find out, didn't we?"

"Find out what?" Buck said huskily.

Martha's throat tightened a little. "I know what I had to find out, dad. That you were right, and that you always had been! That Britt Bannister was the same sneaking, lying man that his father was! That he is a killer like you said all Bannisters were. I found that out!"

Buck looked up at his daughter. He reached up and took her hand and drew her down to him. He put his arm around her then and said gently, "We call that experience, honey. Sometimes it's bought dearer than that."

Martha smiled a little and looked over at Webb.

"Thank you for trying to hide it, but it doesn't matter now. I was wrong, that's all."

Buck presently said to Webb, "Maybe I was wrong about that part, Cousins. But you can't deny you were here when the place was burned and took a part in it."

CHAPTER TWENTY-ONE

Webb told him what his part had been. He told him, too, of the guards he had, and of his plot to bring them here. It was foolish, he admitted, but he had had a wild hope that he might do something to prevent the plundering of the place. He had succeeded in escaping from his guards, but the arrival of Charley upon the scene had been too sudden. Charley had not asked questions; he had simply opened up. And Webb couldn't explain the truth when he regained consciousness, for it would only have meant that Bannister, who was present, would have taken him home to a greater punishment.

Buck listened to this carefully. Webb could see that Buck almost wanted to believe it, but his judgment would not let him. And Webb saw, too, that his story, told as he had just done, seemed lame, evasive, too glib.

It was then that Martha began to ask questions. She asked Webb how he rode over here. Had he been a prisoner? Had he been tied? What had happened when he got here? Webb told her that the hard cases had left him tied on his horse, but with a whisky bottle in his hand. He told how he managed to escape, how he ran down to the house; how, weaponless, he had picked up the rock and hit Shorty with it, afterward getting Shorty's gun. The rest, he said, she had seen for herself.

"But didn't the man you shot ask you to give him a hand?" Martha asked.

"What else could he do?" Webb told her. "He saw I had a gun, and that I had the drop on him. He had to be friendly, pretend to share the loot with me until he caught me off my guard."

Martha turned to her father and told him what she had found.

"It's true, dad. Everything he has said checks with the tracks and what I had guessed."

Buck said nothing. He only sat there staring down at his folded hands. A man could not change his convictions in a few moment's time, nor through listening to talk, no matter how convincing.

Martha finally said, "Dad, I think we've been wrong. Can't you see it?"

Buck did not answer. He turned to Webb. "Why did you come over with this news? You had a chance to escape, to jump the country."

Webb looked steadily at Tolleston, a trace of a smile on his face. "That'll be the hardest part of the whole thing to explain, Tolleston. You won't believe it. Do you want to hear it?"

"Yes."

Looking at the fire, Webb began to talk in a low voice. "When you had me arrested, Tolleston, I had you pegged for a salty devil that wasn't always right, but that was always fair with folks. You were as fair with me as you could be, I reckon, under the circumstances. I liked Wardecker, too. And I didn't like what happened to you-all. I mean about the bank. But I went along. I had to, you might say, but it wasn't all that, either. I took your hoorawin' because I sort of liked you, and I figured that when Stoop came back, he'd put things right.

"But when I run into this business with your daughter and young Bannister, the thing was taken clean out of my hands. I found out things then. First thing that happened to me, I was thrown under the guard of the

five men that held up the bank. I knew then your hunch
about Wintering County was right. And I learned the
worst thing you could say about Bannister wouldn't be
bad enough. He's a crook with a good brain, but he
never had a conscience."

He paused and looked at Tolleston. "Does that sound
phony to you?"

"Go on," Buck said.

"When I tried to break away by comin' up here, and
when I was taken back and thrown in jail, I kept my
eyes and my ears open." He looked at Martha now, meeting her gaze steadily. "The first thing I learned was that
Britt Bannister hated your girl, and that he tried to hire
three of these Montana hardcases to kill you," Webb
said in a low voice. "I'm sorry about that, Miss Martha,
but I was as wrong about him as you. I liked him."

Martha nodded faintly.

Webb continued: "And then I learned about Mitch
Budrow. I figured that he was the one that sold out on
you, and I was sure of it when Wake Bannister hired
these three men to kill him. He knew too much." Webb
paused, almost at a loss for something to say. Then he
said, "Put yourself in my place, Tolleston. Could you
have helped but take sides?"

"Maybe not," Buck said gently.

"I couldn't. I wanted to get out of there, to lay hands
on Mitch Budrow and take him to you. I got out and
I got hold of Mitch, but when I talked to him, I learned
that what he'd done wouldn't be anything to what Bannister was plannin' to do. So I came up."

"Did—did you kill Mitch?" Martha asked.

Webb shook his head. "No. He couldn't go back to
Bannister, because Bannister was tryin' to kill him, and
he knew it. He couldn't come back here, because he'd be
lynched. All he could do was run, and not very far at
that. Bannister'll cook up a charge and put five thousand

on his head and he'll be killed in some town before the
month is up. I figured he'd dug his own grave." He raised
his hands and shrugged. "That's my story, Tolleston.
You can believe it or not."

Buck said nothing, only searched his face, as if something there would tell him if the man was telling the
truth.

Webb saw it was time to play his last card. He said,
"There's one way you can check up on my story, Tolleston."

"What's that?"

"Wait. First, you'll admit that I haven't laid a trap
for you, have I? I haven't told you anything that, if you
believe it, you'd get in more trouble, have I?"

Tolleston thought a moment. Finally he said, "No.
Not that I can see."

"And I have told you somethin' that, if it's true, and
you fight it, you'll be able to whip Bannister. Isn't that
right?"

"That's right."

"All right. You ride into Wagon Mound tonight. I
don't know where a man can put up there, but things
are so the people would know if a stranger came in—
this stranger by the name of Clay Bogardus. That will be
the name of Bannister's agent."

Buck did not hesitate a second. He rose, turned to
Chuck, and said, "Saddle up, Chuck. We're ridin'."

To Webb he said, "I dunno why, son, but I want to
trust you. But I wanted to trust Mitch Budrow, too."

And that, Webb understood, was an apology, and at
the same time a promise. If Bogardus was there, and his
description jibed with the one Webb had from Mitch,
then Webb would be believed. That was all he wanted.

Martha watched Chuck hunt up a lantern, and then
he and Tolleston headed for the rebuilt corral, after
telling Charlie to call in the guards.

When Buck was gone, Martha glanced over at Webb. He was sitting quietly staring into the fire, as if content to be judged. For a moment Martha found herself comparing him with Britt. He had neither Britt's polish nor his good looks, but he had something that Britt never would have, Martha thought—an absolute self-reliance and integrity that events would never change.

She rose then and crossed over to him and held out her hand.

"I believe you without any more proof," she said quietly.

Webb accepted her hand almost shyly. "When I rode up here I wasn't sure if I'd get shot or horsewhipped."

"Dad believes you. He's just thorough."

"He should be," Webb said.

Martha said softly and vehemently, "Oh, this is all so ugly. I wonder if any of us will ever put our trust in anyone again."

She saw Webb watching her, his face grave. "You've got a right to wonder," he said.

Martha knew he was referring to Britt and to the bitter disillusionment he knew she felt. She asked on impulse, "What's happened to Britt, Webb? Why has he turned against me so?"

Webb only shook his head. "I don't know."

"You heard him that day you were eavesdropping on us. How do you square it with what he's done?"

"I don't," Webb said, and added softly, "Some day, though, I hope to square it with him."

"You hate him?"

"Only for what he's done to you," Webb said.

"Why should you care?"

Webb was silent a long moment, looking at her. "I could be shy about this, but I won't be. I think you're good and I think you're decent and friendly and honest and I think a man would be lucky to have you for a wife." He shrugged faintly. "Britt's forgotten that, if he ever knew it. He's gone sour and he's gone wrong and he's tried every way he can to hurt you. That's why I want to square things."

"I wish you wouldn't," Martha said quietly.

Webb held her glance. "Any special reason?"

"Because if you did, I'd be no better than Britt, would I?" She watched Webb consider this, watched him reject it, and knew that Webb believed she still loved Britt.

"You're right," he said, but his words held no conviction, only politeness.

Martha said, almost reluctantly, "Besides, I suppose I'm sentimental. I keep remembering what he once was. Maybe he'll be that way again."

"To you?"

Martha looked at him swiftly. "Not to me, Webb. I'll never give him the chance."

"All right," Webb said. "It's whatever you want."

Martha knew he did not believe her, but before she could ask him, Tolleston called over to Webb to get his horse and come along.

CHAPTER TWENTY-TWO

W<small>EBB HAD NOT SLEPT</small> for a night and a day, but he did not feel tired. He rode between Tolleston and Chuck, and there was not much talk. Tolleston had not asked for his gun, and Webb did not wear it.

Tolleston did not want to talk, and neither did Webb. His thoughts kept returning to Martha Tolleston, and he could not puzzle out the meaning of what she had told him. She had been hurt and humiliated by Britt's treatment of her. Yet she had asked that he be spared when a showdown came. To Webb that meant only one thing, that she still loved Britt Bannister. Women, Webb thought gloomily, were unpredictable. If given a chance, she would probably throw herself at Britt again. The thought made him unreasonably angry, and he tried to banish it from his mind. He had meant every admiring word he had said to Martha. In return she had asked him to spare a man who had wanted to destroy everything she held dear.

He was startled out of his reverie by Buck's strangely gentle voice. "A man never knows his own blood, does he?"

"Hardly ever," Webb replied after a moment's thought. "I reckon he believes in them and lets it go at that."

Buck said nothing. A moment later, he said, "If I had told her more, perhaps this would never have happened."

"She's got a mind of her own. It likely wouldn't have

changed her."

"I mean about Bannister. Why I hate him."

"Why do you?" Webb asked. "What started it—if it's any of my business?"

"That's so long ago, I'd have to think," Buck said slowly. "I remember we never liked each other. We settled in the Big Bend country about the same time, and we both started runnin' cattle. We both loved the same woman at one time. Wake won her, too."

Webb did not comment as Tolleston ceased talking. He knew that there was more to come, and that a man like Tolleston would never let that shape his life.

"It was after he married," Buck said suddenly. "He borrowed money from the Tollestons—some of my kin— to spread out. He wanted more cattle, more riders, more range. You could see he wanted to be on top of the heap, and even then he didn't care much how he got there. He swung a wide loop, but then all of us did in them days, though not so wide as Wake did. He was headstrong too, and didn't care about a man's friendship. He would have lost a friend gladly if he could turn a dollar on it, because dollars meant power. And then one day, a nester, a man Wake had fought with, was found dead, murdered. Wake was arrested, but every man knew that Wake Bannister didn't do it."

"Didn't, you say?" Webb asked.

"Didn't. He was different then. He would have gagged at a murder like any other decent man. Some folks, his enemies, claimed he did it. I claimed he didn't, and the day after the trial, when Wake was convicted and sentenced to six years in the Federal pen, I took a sack of jerky and saddled my horse and went out to do some detectin' myself. I aimed to find the man that murdered this nester." He added quietly, "I'd have done that for Wake's wife."

"Did you find him?"

"I lost his trail in Mexico City," Buck said. "I come back, then. When I got home, I found that my kin had got stampeded when Wake was jailed, and they tried to save the money they had loaned him. They got a quick foreclosure on his spread and threw his wife—Lola—out. Folks said she was goin' to have a baby."

Webb said, "You fixed that up."

"I tried, God knows I tried," Buck said bitterly. "I horsewhipped the man responsible. And then I spent the next five years tryin' to find her, and make it good. I never did find her. Afterward I learned she slaved away in a little border cantina owned by a Mex and lost her health—and later her life."

"And that's what started Bannister?"

"Yes. He blamed me. He always had. When he got out of jail, he was a killer. He sent for his kin. They were outlaws, to a man. They raided my herds, all our herds, killin' night-herders, stampedin' cattle, shootin' in the back, burnin'. It got so a man would ride out of town after a drink, and they'd never see him again. I pulled out, then, and come up here."

"To Wintering?"

"Yes. The Dollar brand was mine. Wake Bannister and all his kin followed me. I was married then. I had a boy, just big enough to fork a gentle pony. He used to ride with me, and when I'd let him, he'd ride with the men. He used to like one hand especially, a line rider. He'd go out and ride line with him and camp with him."

Buck's voice had gradually taken on a hard timbre, but he went on doggedly. "Bannister had just started raidin' my herds then. He raided one one night and stampeded a whole herd over an open camp—the camp my boy was sleepin' in. We found the body of the line rider. It was tromped, but not so bad you couldn't see where he'd been shot in the back. So we knew they'd got to him before they drove the cattle over him."

Webb said gently, "But your boy?"

"What could a kid do?" Tolleston said bitterly. "He climbed a tree, a cedar. The tree was tromped into splinters."

"How did you find that out?" Webb asked.

He could not see Buck Tolleston look at him, but he could almost feel it.

"Because the minute before I killed the man who helped stampede the herd, the man who shot my line rider, he told me he saw the boy climb it, so the boy could have been saved. He died claimin' Bannister never give the order. I know different."

Webb said nothing.

"It almost killed my wife. It did, after Martha was born. That's what Wake wanted."

They rode in silence for a long while. Webb finally said, "Maybe it's better Martha doesn't know it."

"That's what I figured," Buck said quietly. "Now, I'm not so sure. The trouble is, she don't know she ever had a brother. Maybe it's better."

"Maybe it is."

Tolleston did not speak again until they reached Wagon Mound. Then he said to Webb, "You won't believe this when you see it," and Webb thought he seemed calmer. His voice was less harsh than Webb had ever heard it, and Webb wondered if Buck Tolleston had been storing this up within him for all these years. Tonight he had unbent enough to ask advice, like a bewildered old man. Webb felt sorry for him, and understood many things that otherwise he never would have.

There were a few scattered campfires visible in Wagon Mound. As they rode through the town, Webb saw that already some of the ruins were being cleared away. Several tent communities had already been thrown up, but Buck passed these and headed for the four corners. There, where the sheriff's office used to be, was a tent. It was dark inside and Buck did not call out.

They dismounted and Buck went in alone. In a few seconds a lamp was lighted and Buck opened the fly to bid Webb and Chuck enter.

Wardecker was just pulling on his trousers. He smiled and Webb put out a hand.

"Howdy, son."

"Hello, sheriff."

Wardecker said, "Now, Buck, just what is it you want me to do?"

Buck began by telling him the news of the railroad coming in. Wardecker heard it out in blank amazement, but Buck talked on. Forgetting to put on his boots, Wardecker listened, while Webb prompted Buck every so often. When Buck was finished Wardecker swiveled his gaze to Webb.

"Cousins, if this is true, I reckon nothin' we can do for you would show you how we felt. But if it ain't, then lynchin's too good for you." He smiled under his ragged mustache, and Webb knew that the sheriff wanted to believe, along with Buck, but that a hard-bought pessimism prevented their belief.

"I reckon I know where this agent'll be," Wardecker said. "Iron Hat has started a tent hotel down by his windmill. Yesterday a keg of whisky come up on the stage, so I reckon there'll be a game on tonight. You wait here."

He got Webb's description of Bogardus. Added to the fact that he had seen Bogardus himself, Webb had been careful to get a full and clear description of the man from Mitch.

Wardecker hobbled out into the night and headed up street for Iron Hat's tent camp. He could see the fire burning brightly in front of the row of tents where the windmill tower used to stand. Most of the tents were lighted, and from one, as Wardecker drew closer, he would hear the hum of voices, the clatter of poker chips, and the slap of cards. Over the door of this tent was a crudely lettered cardboard sign announcing that this was the *O. K. Saloon.*

Wardecker pulled up the flap and hobbled inside, a scowl on his face. Iron Hat, his green derby riding back on his ears, was dealing a game of poker with five other men. Behind him a barrel of whisky sat in the tent corner. Across the back a board had been laid on two empty barrels for a crude bar. Iron Hat was the barkeep and the house man all in one, and he seemed to be enjoying himself.

At Wardecker's entrance, Iron Hat glanced up.

"Well, well," he growled. "Ain't you old folks afraid of the night air? Didn't you hear the curfew?"

Wardecker didn't smile. He swung across the room to the bar.

"Pour me out a bottle of that poison, Iron Hat. And give me a shot now."

Iron Hat asked, "Toothache?"

Wardecker nodded. "Hurry it up. I'm damned if I think the top of my head'll stay on long enough to let you pour it."

So far, Wardecker had not even glanced at the poker game. Now a player volunteered, "Try tobacco, Will. It fixes mine."

Wardecker shook his head and looked at the man. "I'd rather have the toothache."

Iron Hat set the drink out and Wardecker gulped it down. Then, still scowling, he leaned on the bar to wait for Iron Hat to fill a bottle. He knew all the men here except one. Without settling his gaze on him for more than a second, Wardecker discovered that Webb's description fitted this man to a nicety. Wardecker said over his shoulder to Iron Hat, "Give me another, Iron Hat, and set up the house. I think this is easin' off."

Iron Hat poured drinks all around as Wardecker en-

gaged in small talk with one of the poker players. As
Iron Hat dealt out the drinks, he gestured to the stranger.

"This is Clay Bogardus, Will." And to Bogardus, he
said, "If that stuff curdles in the glass, it's because Wardecker bought a round. Me, if I didn't know the whisky,
I wouldn't drink it. I'd think there was somethin' phony."
Then he gestured to Wardecker, smiling a little. "That's
the sheriff, Will Wardecker. Don't ask, 'Sheriff of what?'
because it's mainly a dozen tents and a lot of grass. He's
the man that set fire to the town. He was too lazy to
sheriff it."

Wardecker was used to the mild rawhiding he received
from Iron Hat, and he usually gave as good as he took.
But tonight he did not want to appear convivial. He
nodded casually to Bogardus and picked up his bottle,
saying to Iron Hat, "Well, my toothache's gone. So are
my teeth, I reckon, after that drink. Good night, boys."

He swung out through the fly and hobbled off into the
night. Back in his own tent, he set the whisky down and
looked at Buck.

"The man is Bogardus, and he tallies up with the description."

Buck said, "Then we ride for Hasker. You better come
later, Wardecker—let us ride out first."

They waited on the edge of town until Wardecker
joined them. The sheriff, in spite of his lame leg, sat a
horse as well as the next man, and he carried his crutch
rammed in the saddle boot. They headed west. Although
Buck had not said as much, Webb knew that they believed him now and that he was one of them.

They arrived at the Chain Link just as the east was
graying. The buildings were situated at the far end of a
box canyon, whose high walls gave it and the corrals
ample shelter from the weather. The entrance to the box
Canyon was narrow, but the canyon itself widened out

as they went deeper into it.

By the dim morning light Webb could see that the Chain Link had once been an impressive place, if a man was to judge by the area covered with blackened ashes. The house itself had gone the same way as Tolleston's. It had been a spacious one-story stone affair under spreading trees, but now it was a black, roofless, windowless hulk. Off against the side of the canyon was the long adobe bunk house, typical of these ranches. Its roof was still on, and a thick streamer of smoke was issuing from the cook-shack chimney. Dim lights could be seen at the end of the bunk house itself.

A shadowy figure challenged them from the awninged porch of the bunk house, and Wardecker answered, "It's me, Frank. We want to see Lou."

"More trouble?" the man asked, walking up to their horses, holding his rifle slack in his hand.

"No, but I reckon there will be. How is Lou?"

"Doin' good. He's asleep, I reckon. You want to wake him?"

"Yes. This is important, Frank."

"Get down and come on," the foreman said.

They walked down the long awninged porch to its far end.

"He's sleepin' in his office, now," Frank said. He opened the door and walked in, the others following.

Hasker wakened to ask who it was, and Frank said, "Company, Lou. Plenty of it."

"Light the lamp," Hasker said.

As the match flared up and the lamp was lighted, Webb made out a man lying in a bed against the far corner. He was a redhead, hardly older than Webb himself, but his face was beard-stubbled and drawn, pale against the lamplight. He raised himself up on an elbow and blinked at the room, then he smiled.

"Howdy, boys. What's the party?"

Wardecker said, "How you feel, Lou? Wide awake enough to listen close?"

"Sure." He spoke to his foreman. "Tell Mose to rustle up some food, Frank, in a hurry."

"No time, Lou," Buck put in.

"He's got coffee made, sure. Tell him to bring that in, Frank."

The foreman went out and Buck introduced Webb to Hasker. They shook hands, Hasker surveying Webb with a quizzical expression on his face.

Wardecker saw it and said, "Yes, that's Webb, the prisoner. Listen to what he's got to say."

So for the third time that night, Webb told his story. He told it from the beginning, and did not even stop when the cook brought in a huge pot of coffee and tin cups. The rest of them did not drink either, for they were listening, too.

As the story unfolded, Hasker sat up, and his eyes never left Webb's face. Occasionally he asked a question, but mostly he listened and there was growing incredulity on his face as Webb progressed and finished.

Webb sat back when he was done, and let Hasker ask all the questions he wanted.

Finally Hasker turned to Wardecker. "You say you saw this man Bogardus, Will? He's in town now?"

"Yes, and if what Cousins says is true, he'll be huntin' me up some time this mornin'."

Hasker looked over at Webb. "That sounds true," he said slowly. "I don't know you, don't know anything about you, but it sounds like Bannister." He smiled a little at Buck. "And he was right, Buck. I'd made up my mind to sell and pull out."

"You would have sold for seventy thousand?"

"Gladly."

Hasker told Frank, a heavy-set, middle-aged man with bowed legs and a leathery tough face, to pour out the coffee. He did, and they drank in silence, then lighted up pipes and cigarettes.

Hasker settled back against the wall. "Well, we've got him finagled now, boys. What'll we do with him?"

Webb set his coffee cup down on the table and swung his chair to the floor. "Wait a minute," he said quietly, looking at them all. "I'd like to know one thing before you start to talk. I want to hear you say it."

"What's that?" Buck asked.

"I want to know if you believe what I've told. If you don't, I want you to say so, and I'll ride out of here today. But if you do, I want you to tell me. I want to know another thing, too."

Buck spoke for himself. "I believe you, Cousins. I believe every damned word of it." The others seconded him. "What's the other thing?"

"I want you to listen to one thing I've got to say," Webb went on. "It's come to me in the last half hour that you've got a way to nail Bannister down—nail him and skin him. I wondered if you want to hear it."

"Shoot."

So Webb told them, and they listened.

When he was finished, Buck Tolleston cleared his throat. "It couldn't be neater," he said flatly. "I'm for it, and I'm for it all the way. All it takes is some careful work on your part, Wardecker. Cousins will do his part. He can't help it."

"And you can be in the next room to check up on me," Webb said.

"I don't even want to," Wardecker said.

"Nor me," Hasker said.

Webb looked around him. "Gents," he said, "I've got a little debt of my own to square here. I'm just ornery enough to like to square it this way."

And all of them laughed.

CHAPTER TWENTY-THREE

BOGARDUS ran down Wardecker by noon. Wardecker was superintending the digging of a well west of town where the water was sure to be safe. Wagons loaded with timber had begun to trickle in from the mountains that morning, and the work of reconstructing the town was beginning.

The new town would be built west of the old. The prairie was flat, and there was space all around. Therefore, since there was no sense in clearing away ashes to build, it had been decided to move the town over. Men with shovels and picks were digging foundations just east of the well. Wardecker was helping rig a frame for the buckets to be hauled up on when he noticed Bogardus watching the work.

When he was finished, Wardecker backed off and packed his pipe, never looking at Bogardus.

A voice, Bogardus's voice, made him look up. The big man was standing beside him, surveying the work.

"That's a heartbreakin' job," Bogardus observed.

"Do us good," Wardecker said, his face amiable. "We had a hell of a town. We'll have a better one."

Bogardus nodded. "You remember me, sheriff?"

Wardecker looked at him. "Can't say I do, exactly. But I meet lots of people."

"Last night," Bogardus said. "You came into Iron Hat Petty's."

"Oh, sure, sure. Them teeth was givin' me fits. I wouldn't have remembered meetin' my mother. How are you?"

They talked idly this way for a few minutes and then Bogardus came down to business.

"Look here, sheriff. I'm goin' to ask you a favor. If what I'm about to say ain't any of my business, just tell me."

"Shoot."

"I'm a cattleman down south," Bogardus began. "We heard down there about this fight you folks have had with Winterin' County next door. We even heard about the burnin'. From the train crew."

"Sure."

"Now here's what ain't any of my business. Is it true that a lot of these ranchers here in this county are aimin' to pull out, sellin' their places?"

Wardecker snorted. "That's anybody's business. Sure it's true. And I don't blame 'em. Why?"

Bogardus tipped back his hat and smiled. "Well, it's kind of hard to explain, Wardecker. You see, it's this way. I got a little money and I want to spread out. The way I figured it, my money would go further if I bought a place from a man willin' to sell than if I bought from a man I had to pry loose from a place he liked."

Wardecker looked sharply at him. "You mean you want to buy a place here?"

"That's about it, if they're worth buyin', and they want to sell."

"You'll be buyin' right smack dead center into the middle of a feud, mister," Wardecker said flatly, a feigned expression of wonder on his face.

"I thought of that. I thought of it a lot. But it don't make much difference. The way I figure it, these men over in Winterin' don't know me, and they couldn't have anything agin' me. I mind my own business and they'll mind theirs."

He shrugged. "Of course, if they want a fight, then I aim to give 'em one. But I don't see why they should. Accordin' to what I've heard, it's just you old-timers that hate each other."

"Any Winterin' man hates any San Patricio man," Wardecker said.

"Maybe. But I aim to do it different." He laughed. "I'm bull-headed, you might say. I want to find out for myself."

"If you buy a place, you'll git plenty chance."

"That's all I want."

Wardecker lighted his pipe again and frowned, as if trying to think.

"Just what places is for sale?" Bogardus asked. "I'd like to know."

"How big?"

"Pretty big," Bogardus said. "If a man's goin' to gamble, there's no use gamblin' for white chips."

"This ain't a gamble," Wardecker said. "But you asked for it." He hesitated. "There's several sizable spreads whose owners would like to pull out. The reason you ain't heard of them is likely because they never thought there'd be many—many—"

"Suckers like me?" Bogardus finished for him, chuckling.

"Suckers like you," Wardecker echoed, grinning also. "But I've heard Frank Winterhoven over west say that he'd like to sell. I've heard Mrs. Anders over by Buck Tolleston would like to pull out if she could. Lou Hasker over at the Chain Link has been cleaned out by that bank robbery. He'd like to sell, too. Maybe Miles Kindry's widow would, but that's a mighty big spread. Maybe bigger'n you want."

"How big are these places?" Bogardus asked.

"You'd ought to see 'em," Wardecker said.

"I aim to. You know a man around here I could take with me to show me around? I'd almost need him."

Wardecker frowned. "Every able-bodied man in town is workin' now." He looked up at Bogardus. "What about me? I ain't no damn use around a bunch of well diggers."

Bogardus demurred. "No, I wouldn't like to ask that, Wardecker. You'll be busy."

Wardecker then chuckled softly. "When I was swore into office, I took a oath to protect the people of this county. Protectin' means helpin', don't it? All right, if I help, say, Mrs. Anders to get rid of the Seven A, then I'll be protectin' her, won't I?"

Bogardus's lean face creased in a smile. "That's one way of lookin' at it."

"All right. Let's go get horses." Wardecker looked at his watch. "We only got a half day left. We'll hit for Winterhoven over west and talk to him and stay the night. Tomorrow, we'll drift over to the Chain Link and from there across to the Seven A. That'll take a full day. Then we'll—"

"But I don't aim to take up a week of your time, sheriff," Bogardus protested.

"I'm glad to do a man a favor," Wardecker said. "Come along."

They arrived at Winterhoven's that afternoon. Bogardus talked with Frank Winterhoven, and rode over a section of the range with him.

They discussed cattle and water and taxes and shelter and grass and prices, and from it all, Wardecker gathered that Bogardus was a plenty shrewd cattleman. He knew his business, and he knew what he wanted. And never once did he show a lack of interest in what Winterhoven was showing him.

They stayed the night there, and the next morning they left Winterhoven with promises to consider his terms.

The sheriff had told Winterhoven nothing of Bogardus's identity, so that Winterhoven's actions were natural and easy.

The Chain Link adjoined Winterhoven's place, and it was only a short ride between them.

CHAPTER TWENTY-FOUR

Approaching the Chain Link spread, Wardecker said to Bogardus, "Lou Hasker owns this place. He's young, and a good rancher. He'll be glad to pull out of here, I reckon, while he still is young, and move somewhere where his neighbors is a little whiter." He motioned to his leg. "You see, Hasker got shot in that scrap at Bull Foot. Right here. He's laid up in bed and he's likely fed up with the whole business."

They dismounted at the bunk house. Bogardus looked over the ruins of the old house and shook his head.

"They mean business over there in Wintering, don't they?"

Wardecker said they did. He led the way down to the office and knocked on the door. A voice bade him enter.

Wardecker stepped aside for Bogardus, who had to lower his head to clear the door. Bogardus adjusted his eyes to the gloom of the room and saw a man lying in a bed in the corner.

"Howdy, Will," the man said.

"Hello, Lou. How goes it?"

"Poco-poco. How's it with you?"

"Good. Lou, this is Clay Bogardus, a cattleman from over south."

As Bogardus walked across to shake hands with the man, he observed him carefully. He was redheaded, lean, freckle-faced, with rain-gray piercing eyes, and a rather wide mouth that wore an engaging grin.

"Glad to meet you, Bogardus. This is a hell of a way to wecome a man—from a bed. I feel like a honkytonk gal."

They all laughed and the redhead bade them be seated.

Wardecker lighted up his pipe and after some small talk said, "Lou, Bogardus here is lookin' for to buy a place. He heard about the feud, but it don't mean much to him. I told him I'd heard you say you wanted to sell the Chain Link and pull out. What about it?"

The redhead looked at Bogardus. "A buyer, huh? Sure, I want to pull out, Bogardus. If I can't sell it, I'd almost give it away. I got a bellyful of this war. I'm pullin' out before they nail my hide up."

"That's what Wardecker said."

"Sure. You look around. I'll send a man out with you and you can look at every foot of my range. It's a fair range, it's got good water, and there's lots of it. It ain't got a house, and it won't have many cattle in another two months if I keep it and if I know Bannister. You still interested?"

"Enough to look at it."

"Good. Will, give a shout for Frank."

Wardecker opened the door and called the foreman. Presently Frank entered and was introduced to Bogardus.

He got his orders. "Take Bogardus around the place, Frank. You goin' too, Will?"

"Sure. Been many a month since I rode across your range, Lou."

"Good. Take 'em both, Frank." And then he grinned. "And don't lie, Frank. You don't have to. Bogardus must be crazy to begin with."

Bogardus laughed and rose. Frank showed him out along with the sheriff. Presently, as soon as the redhead heard them ride off, he got up and walked to the window. The door from the bunk house opened and Buck Tolleston stepped in.

"Well?" Buck said, grinning.

"You heard it, didn't you?"

"Enough to know he swallowed it, Webb."

Webb Cousins was in bed again when, toward dusk, Wardecker and Bogardus returned to the house.

"Go get supper first," Webb said. "A man can't talk on an empty stomach."

After they had eaten, they returned to the office, which was lighted now by the small table lamp. Bogardus rolled his after-supper smoke and inhaled luxuriously.

"How does the place stack up?" Webb asked. "Suit you?"

Bogardus nodded. "If we can come to terms, Hasker, I think I'll buy. I can't see a thing wrong with it."

"Except the neighbors across the line," Webb said.

"I'll take care of that. If you'll give me an idea of your count, I'll make you an offer. When I take over, of course, I'll settle the count right."

Webb thought a moment. "The place as it stands is worth eighty thousand. That's countin' every head of cattle on the place accordin' to my last book tally, and figurin' them at considerable below market prices. You know why I'm doin' that, don't you?"

"Because you can't ship without a loss?"

"Yes. Then eighty thousand. The bank holds my note for thirty thousand and they'll give me all the time I want to meet it." He thought a moment. "You can take over everything—my note, too—for forty thousand dollars. Or you can take it without the note for seventy thousand."

Bogardus said cautiously, "What terms?"

Webb didn't want to appear too lenient. "Those are cash terms, Bogardus. If you won't take it, I reckon I'll stay here and fight."

Bogardus got out a pencil and a piece of paper and

spent five minutes figuring in silence. When he looked up, he said, "I'll take it. I'd like a little time on ten thousand of it, if you can see it that way."

Webb shook his head. "Huh-uh. Cash on the barrel head. I want to get out of here and I never want to hear of the damn place again."

Bogardus shrugged. "All right. That suits me."

Webb grinned and held out his hand. "Brother, take over. When do you move in?"

"As soon as I can. I'll see your banker tomorrow about those notes. Then I'll be out with cash and a notary public and a deed."

Webb nodded at the sheriff. "Wardecker's a notary. Bring him out. He'll help you with what you need in town. Anything else?"

"Not that I can think of. After we sign, I'll head south and send my men up. Will you be ready to move out right away?"

"Tomorrow, I can travel. I'll turn the keys over to you tomorrow morning. What about my men?" When he saw Bogardus frown, he grinned. "Don't be afraid to say it, Bogardus. The only reason they've stuck in this shootin' gallery is on account of me."

"I'll bring my own, then," Bogardus said.

Webb nodded. Wardecker and Bogardus stood up, and, after Webb had given Wardecker instructions to have Tolleston show Bogardus the books, they bade him good night and went out.

Once they were clear of the place, Webb rose and pulled on his boots. Tolleston entered as he was doing so. Neither spoke to the other, for Buck had heard every word from beneath the open window in back. They only smiled at each other.

Together they carried Hasker in from the well house, where he had spent the day, and put him in bed. He listened to the story of the deal with a grin on his face.

"Good. Bannister has curled his tail just once too often," Hasker said.

Afterward, in his blankets in the bunk house, Webb lay there awake, trying to find a flaw in the plan. He could not, but he scarcely dared admit it to himself.

Buck's voice came through the dark. "Tomorrow, son, I start ridin'. And for the last time. Because if it don't go through, we can't ride again. If it does, we won't have to."

CHAPTER TWENTY-FIVE

Bogardus rode into the Chain Link in mid-morning, alongside Sheriff Wardecker. The conference with Webb, again in bed in Hasker's place, was brief and to the point.

"I found everything like you said," Bogardus said. "I'm ready to sign. I'll take over everything—notes and all."

Webb sent Wardecker to call two hands to witness the deed. It was signed and witnessed and stamped by Wardecker and given to Bogardus, who counted out forty thousand dollars in Federal banknotes and gave them to Webb, who let them lie on the bed.

"I'll be moved out this afternoon, Bogardus," Webb said. "So come when you like. I'll leave the cook here. You can keep him or pay him off when you move in."

Bogardus thanked him. The straight-faced, casual acting of the man was something to enjoy. When Bogardus got ready to go, he put the deed in his pocket and came over to the bed to shake hands.

"I think I got a bargain, Hasker," he said, smiling a little.

"That's accordin' to the way you look at it," Webb said, taking his hand.

"Watch that leg. So long, and good luck," Bogardus said.

Wardecker rode out with him, saying that a man who carried a deed to that much property should have some protection with him.

Webb rose and, calling one of the hands, brought Hasker in again. Then Hasker's remaining hands assembled in the room and Hasker told them what had happened, down to the last detail of the plot. These were men to be trusted, men who had fought with Hasker, and when they heard this plan which would enable them to revenge the death of so many of their companions, a subtle change came over them. Webb could see it in their faces. Instead of men who were sticking to an unpleasant job out of loyalty to a friend, they were men who saw a chance for revenge and a fighting one.

Hasker told them that from now on, they were to take orders from Webb.

"We've got to make a camp up in the Frying Pans," Webb said briefly. "That camp, we hope, will have to hold about thirty men for at least a week. By tonight, I want this place deserted. More than that, I don't want a man to ride into it again until he has orders. Now come to me for your jobs."

They were simple. Food had to be hauled, meat butchered, bedding and pots taken in round-up wagon, horses moved over to a corral in the foothills, and all of it done this day.

By that evening the camp was established in a small hidden canyon of the Frying Pans. It was hardly completed before men began to drift in. Buck Tolleston had been riding once again to muster a fighting crew. But this time he had something to offer them and they came. Ranchers brought their whole outfits, deserting their spreads. Nesters, townspeople, all chosen men, all men with a score to settle, gathered here. They trickled in all during the night and none of them brought their womenfolks. It was to be war to the finish, this time.

Webb slept that night, too, but by early morning he took Chuck Martin aside and was giving him orders.

"Mind, I don't say it'll be today, but I think it will.

Bannister will send a rider over to check up on us, to see if we've moved. I want that rider spotted. I want to know he's been there. Do you think we can do it?"

Martin nodded and departed.

Men kept riding in all during that day, and Webb saw that, to a man, they came prepared for trouble. Carbines were in saddle boots that had never known a gun. Extra shell-belts, cracked and dusty, were dug up and worn. Case after case of rifle shells were brought. And, strangely, these men were quiet, sober, but it was a false quiet.

That night Buck Tolleston rode in with Wardecker, and a council was held. Buck explained in detail what had happened during the past week, and how this plan had been worked out to perfection.

"Wake Bannister will wait a day or so—that'll be today, we hope—and then he'll move in. He'll move in with a whole crew—a crew of gun-dogs and saddle bums and fightin' men. We'll be there to meet him. That's the whole plan."

He named off a dozen men. "You men will guard that bottle neck to the canyon. Once they're past you, I want the trap closed. The rest of us will be inside the bunk house behind locked doors. Wake Bannister will have his chance. He'll surrender and hang, or he'll fight and die. And"—Buck's voice was calm and sober—"I hope he elects to fight."

He looked around the campfire. "There are five of us won't be in the bunk house with you—Lou Hasker, Webb Cousins, Frank Winterhoven, Will Wardecker, and myself. We'll talk to Bannister."

"What are we waitin' for?" a man asked.

"For word that Bannister has sent a man over to make sure Hasker has moved out. When we get that word, we move."

It came later that night. Martin rode in and reported to Buck.

"The man was over," he said. "It looked like Hugo Meeker, from where I watched. He got the key and went through all the buildin's. He talked with the cook, and then he went through 'em again. I reckon he thinks we've gone."

"Did you talk to the cook?" Buck asked.

Martin shook his head. "Not till it was dark. I laid on my belly and never moved for seven hours. Wasn't takin' a chance."

Webb grinned. "What did Meeker say to the cook?"

"He pretended he was a gent out from town to see Hasker. He couldn't believe he'd moved, and claimed the cook lied. But Mose stuck to his story. He claimed it was funny Meeker never saw Hasker in town, because that's where he was goin'. Meeker bullied him around considerable, and then left."

Buck turned to the assembled men. "All right. We move. You know who's to take the horses, how you're to get in the bunk house, so's to guard the bottle neck. One thing. No smoking. No moving around. This place has got to look deserted. One careless smoke and we're discovered. It may be a day before they come. If it is, we'll move back here at night."

They saddled up and rode out of the canyon, forty of them. It was more than Buck had counted on. Better than that, it was not a crowd of rabble raised to a fighting pitch on whisky. It was an orderly band, grim to silence.

They took over the Chain Link before dawn. By sunup, the spread looked deserted. Not a horse in the corrals, not a man, except Mose, who was peeling potatoes in the open door of the cook shack, in sight. There was no sound, no hum of quiet talk. The place looked empty, except for the thin wreath of smoke that curled out of the cook-shack chimney.

In the bunk house, men slept or played quietly at cards, their guns beside them. In the office, Webb and the others sat around the room and tried to be patient. Hasker lay in bed, a cold pipe in his mouth, his eyes dancing with excitement. Occasionally he would look at Webb, this man who had his own red hair and freckles, almost his own build, and was the same age as he was. Hasker knew he had succeeded in his own line, but looking at Webb, that success did not count for so much. Here was a man who had twice his daring, at least his own love of a good fight, and a man who bore an indefinable stamp of leadership about him. He liked him, liked the quick smile, the hard, pleasantly ugly face of him, and the way he acted. He wished he knew more about him.

They could all hear the cook banging around the kitchen, chopping wood, whistling. Morning passed and most of the men were asleep. For lunch they ate jerky and water and sat around and waited. As the afternoon dragged on, Webb felt their tension slack. Bannister would not come today. He thought that himself.

In later afternoon, almost at dusk, he got up and opened the door a little, to let some fresh air in. He was about to turn away when he paused, listening.

Slowly, then, he turned to face the others.

"It's here," he said quietly. "I hear horsemen."

Buck Tolleston leaped for the door of the bunk house. His appearance quieted the hum of talk and, noticing it, the men in the bunks raised up.

"They're here," Buck said. "Get your gun beside you. Keep quiet. Don't make a move until I signal from this doorway."

He closed the door behind him and sat down in his chair.

Webb remained at the crack in the door. The sound of approaching horsemen grew louder until it was directly in the yard.

Webb heard Wake Bannister call, "Black boy, is this

place locked up?"

"That's right, boss," the cook said. "You Mistuh Bo-gardus's men?"

"Where are the keys?" Bannister demanded.

"In the office. That's right down this here porch, right on the end. On 'at table, boss."

Slowly Webb closed the door and tiptoed softly to the foot of the bed and faced the door. Tolleston shifted faintly in his seat and quieted again as the sound of approaching footsteps came to them.

They heard the footsteps pause outside, heard the knob turned. The door opened and Wake Bannister walked in.

Webb watched his face. Not until he was a full step inside the dark room did Wake Bannister notice that there were people in here.

He stopped abruptly and looked around him, and slowly, by a hardening of his jaw line, he betrayed that he knew them. Meeker was behind him, also inside the door now, and his face did not change in the slightest when he looked around the room. A cigarette was pasted to his lower lip. He lounged against the door, thumbs hooked in belt, and smiled arrogantly.

Webb heard Buck rise. Saw him out of the corner of his eye. But Buck didn't speak.

It was Hasker, from the bed, who drawled. "Look at this. What in hell are you doin' here, Bannister? Lookin' for little chickens to kick?"

Bannister ignored him. His gaze settled on Buck.

"A reception committee, eh, Buck?"

"You might call it that," Buck said gently. "But an-swer the question."

Meeker started to straighten up, and Webb said swiftly, "Don't go out there, Meeker. Just relax."

Bannister arrogantly stepped farther into the room. Now he looked at Hasker. "What am I doin' here on the

Chain Link?" he asked firmly. "I might ask you that question." He slowly reached into the inside pocket of his coat and pulled out a paper. "You see, I own it."

"I didn't know I sold it," Hasker said.

Wake extended the paper and Hasker took it.

Wake said, "That, gentlemen, is a bluff that won't work. I have fifty men out here to enforce what I say—and I say 'Get out!' "

No one moved. Only the rustling of the paper was in the room.

Hasker said, "Made out to Clay Bogardus." He looked over the paper at Webb.

"Isn't that the gent that was out here yesterday, Cousins?"

"I think so."

"Isn't he the man you sold the Chain Link to?"

Webb nodded. Hasker folded up the paper and handed it back to Bannister.

"Sorry, Bannister. You see, I didn't sell the Chain Link. The redheaded, freckle-faced man of about twenty-six with the gray eyes and the wide mouth that Bogardus bought the Chain Link from yesterday is that man over there—Webb Cousins."

Bannister just stared at him, and then slowly lifted his gaze to Webb, who was lounging against the wall.

"I happened to be in bed here," Webb drawled quietly. "I just sold him the place, signed the deed, took his money—your money, I mean." He smiled unpleasantly.

"What I'm trying to tell you, you big curly wolf, is that I pretended I was Hasker. The deed you've got to the Chain Link isn't legal, so your heirs will never collect. You don't own it. You and your gunnies out there are trespassin'. It wouldn't make any difference if you weren't. You're in San Patricio County, which is excuse enough for us. Tell him, Wardecker."

Wardecker said quietly, "You're arrested, Bannister,

for the murder of twenty-odd men, for the murder of Mitch Budrow, and for robbing the U. S. mail. You'd better come along peaceful."

Hugo Meeker slowly turned his head and looked out the door, then looked back and yawned.

Wake Bannister smiled slightly.

"Gentlemen, the day when six of you can take me away from fifty men and arrest me hasn't dawned yet."

"Not six of us, Wake," Buck said in ominous gentleness. "This bunk house is packed with men. We're just giving you a chance."

They faced each other now, these enemies of more than two decades. Buck, a head shorter than Bannister, stood straight as a ramrod, his hands at his sides, his blue eyes alight with fire. Bannister met his glance with one as hard and cold as agate.

Buck said slowly, without smiling, "This is payday, Wake. Give up or fight out of it."

Bannister looked over Buck's head to Hugo. There was no signal in that look that Webb could read, but Hugo understood it. Intuitively, Webb did, too.

Meeker started to twist out of the door, his hand already streaking to his gun, when Webb shot. The slug caught Hugo in the side, high in the chest, and spun him around so that he pitched flat on the porch, his gun clattering to the floor.

And in the same split second, Wake Bannister made his choice, too. Hasker saw his hand blur to the gun on his hip. Under the covers, Hasker held a Colt in his own hand, but he did not whip it out. This was Buck Tolleston's fight.

Buck understood that. He dived at Bannister, his hand clenching Bannister's wrist in a grip of iron as Bannister's hand closed on the butt of his gun.

Wake slashed out viciously with his other hand, the brute strength of his blow sending Buck kiting into the

wall. But Buck was smiling when he thudded into the
adobe wall, for he had a gun in his hand.

He shot it empty, laughing, watching Bannister try
with nerveless fingers to claw his gun out of its holster,
and, failing that, turn in strangled fury to lunge at him.
He took one heavy step before his knees folded, and he
toppled face down on the floor.

CHAPTER TWENTY-SIX

WEBB WAS IN THE DOORWAY, a hand raised to the horsemen outside in the dusk who, to a man, had turned in frozen surprise at the sound of the gunfire.

"Bannister and Meeker are dead, you men!" Webb shouted. "We have fifty men here in this bunk house! Will you surrender, or fight and die?"

For answer, a shot from the wing of the circling horsemen smashed into the door sill, and Webb dodged back, but not before he saw the smoke of Britt Bannister's raised gun. Then a mighty fusillade of shots smashed through the doorway.

Buck crashed open the door to the bunk house, but he had no time to speak. The men were piling out of the two doors and the crescendo of gunfire rose until it seemed to rock the earth.

The Bannister riders were at a disadvantage. They were bunched, some still mounted, and the stampede that resulted was a fury of horseflesh and gunshots.

Some tried to break through and turn back, and rode over men in their frantic haste. Others forted down behind shot horses. Still others ran through the deepening dusk for the shelter of the burned house.

Webb flung open the door and dodged to the corner of the house. He picked out the gaudy shirt of Britt Bannister, afoot in that tangle of rearing horses and shooting men.

Recklessly Webb ran for that moil. Britt had fought his way out now and was running for the shelter of the ruined house.

A man shot at Webb from horseback, and Webb smashed his gun across the nose of the horse, which reared back into more milling riders. Now he was in this throng of men who were snarling and cursing and trying to free themselves. He did not shoot. He kept Britt Bannister in sight until he disappeared into the deep shadows of what was left of the burned-out house.

Webb followed him, diving through a door.

"Where's young Bannister?" he asked a man who was firing a rifle through a window.

The man turned. It was Perry Warren. Even as he recognized Webb, he nosed up his rifle and fired blindly. Webb shot and saw him go down, but he did not stop. He dashed into the next room, where a man was scrambling frantically through a window. And on into the next, which was a hall.

Down its dark length he saw someone move.

"Bannister!" Webb called. A racket of shots ripped orange in that darkness, and Webb felt something slam into his leg. He fell, his gun swinging up and exploding twice.

"Come and get me, damn you!" a man snarled. It was Bannister's voice.

Webb loaded his gun, lying there trying not to move more than was necessary. He had this house figured out now. This was the corridor where the stairs climbed to the second story.

The stairs were burned now, a heap of rubbish lying where they had once stood. The corridor, Bannister had obviously discovered, was a dead-end one.

Webb said quietly, "Come out of there with your hands up and you won't get shot, you fool!"

There was no answer. Webb called, "Bannister!"

A shot ripped out and the slug splintered into the rubble beside Webb's head.

"Come out of there!" Webb said. "You won't get shot."

"Did that killer's gal put you up to that?" Bannister taunted.

Webb cursed him, a blind rage boiling up in him. He did not hear the gunfire outside, though it was swelling mightily in the lowering darkness. He called out, "She did, and I don't know why! But I won't shoot you! But if you don't come out of there, I'll come in and take you!"

There was no answer, only a slow moving back in the dark. Suddenly Bannister said, "All right, I'll surrender."

Webb called, "Throw down those guns. Throw 'em loud, so I can hear 'em!"

He counted two distinct crashes of metal on dirt and rock and then he called, from where he lay, "Come out! With your hands up!"

He heard Bannister walking toward him. He could make out an indistinct bulk in the dark, two hands held over the head. Then the footsteps paused, not ten feet ahead of him.

"Where are you?" Bannister asked plaintively.

Webb rose. "Here. Come out and—"

A blast of gunfire cut off his words. He fell to the floor, rolling against the wall. Despairingly he remembered his promise to Martha that Britt would not be killed. There was only one thing to do then and that was to pretend that Britt's treachery had worked. Rolling over on his face, he groaned softly and lay still.

Now he could hear Britt's first tentative step toward him. There were two more steps, and then Britt halted as if uncertain. There was a long silence, and then more confidently Britt moved toward him. Webb heard him halt above him, and now he felt Britt's boot in his side, trying to toe him over. Webb relaxed, giving slackly against the pressure of Britt's boot. It was dark here and

Webb knew that Britt would strike a match to make sure he was dead. The only question was, would he shoot a second time before he struck the match?

The following seconds seemed endless as Webb waited. Now he heard Britt fumbling around in his pockets. There was a pause and Webb gathered himself. He knew that in the first flash of light Britt would be momentarily blinded and that would be the time to act.

Now he listened, and suddenly the rasp of a match being struck came to him. Webb rolled over, lunging for the gun that Britt held slackly at his side. Webb's big hand settled over the cylinder, and then the match died and Britt pulled savagely at his gun.

Webb knew only that he must keep his hand around the cylinder so that the hammer could not fall. He was on his knees now when Britt's savage kick caught him in the side. Webb grunted and now grasped the gun with his other hand. Britt was kicking furiously at him, but in the darkness his kicks were deflected off Webb's thigh.

Kneeling now, both hands on the gun, Webb gathered all his strength and twisted with both hands, at the same time falling to the floor. His weight, combined with the twisting motion, wrenched the gun out of Britt's hands.

On his face now, Webb threw the gun out of the way and then rose to his knees, diving at Britt's legs. Wrapping his arms around Britt's thighs, he drove his body forward, legs pumping. Suddenly he felt Britt smash into the wall. Britt had been slugging blindly, furiously, at his back, but at the impact the blows ceased. With leverage now, Webb lifted and with a mighty heave dumped Britt head first over his shoulder. Webb was half turned when he heard Britt grunt as he hit the floor. Webb dived then and found he was astride Britt's body, and he began slugging wildly.

He could not remember the number of blows he took or gave. All he knew was that Britt bucked him off, that he clung to Britt, that they both rose and were finally erect, facing each other, striking blindly in the dark.

Maneuvering to his right, Webb suddenly saw Britt's form before him framed through a broken window against the lighter sky.

Savagely Webb drove his fist at Britt's head. The blow connected so solidly that the jolt traveled up to Webb's shoulder. Britt took two steps backward and the window sill caught him at the knee. Webb's lunge at him was almost too late, for Britt fell back through the window, Webb on top of him. Once on the ground, Britt did not move. Slowly Webb rose. He was aware now that the firing had ceased and that men were shouting to each other over by the bunk house, which now held a light. Suddenly a running form appeared out of the night in front of him, and he heard a girl's voice call, "Webb! Webb Cousins!"

Webb halted, his heart still thumping wildly. This would be Martha Tolleston, and he knew what her first question would be.

"Here," Webb said. He saw her turn and before he could say more she had run into his arms. She held him tightly, burying her face in his chest, and Webb waited for the question. *Say it,* he thought. *Ask about him.*

"Are you hurt?" Martha asked.

"No," Webb answered coldly. "Neither is he."

Martha raised her head. "Who?"

"Britt. That's what you wanted to know, isn't it?"

There was a stirring at Webb's feet, and he looked down. Slowly Britt Bannister pulled himself to a sitting position, shaking his head. Gently Webb broke away from Martha, then reached down and hauled Bannister to his feet. He could not see the expression on Martha's face, but he said roughly, "There he is. I saved him for you."

Martha was silent, and now Webb turned to Bannister. "Everyone pays up but you," he said bitterly. "There she is and she wants you."

"Do I?" Martha asked, a strange coldness in her voice.

Britt said grimly, "She may want me, but she hasn't got me."

Martha said sharply, "Webb, what are you trying to do?"

"Just what you wanted me to," Webb said bitterly. "Here he is all in one package, a little mussed, but still pretty." He wheeled to walk away.

"Webb," Martha's voice was more imploring than sharp. "Come back here!"

Webb halted and retraced his steps. "This is for you to hear," Martha said. Now she half turned to Bannister. "Tell me something, Britt," she demanded. "What turned you against me so suddenly?"

"You're a Tolleston," Britt said.

"But I always was. You knew that."

"I knew it," Britt said thinly. "Trouble is I didn't know that your father helped kill my mother. I didn't know what trash you were."

"Thank you, Britt," Martha said softly. "For a while I thought we were the only two sane people in both our families. Now I know that I'm the only sane one. At least I'm sane enough that I can't hate you."

"Sure," Britt said derisively. "When do you plan to shoot me?"

At that moment Wardecker's voice called from the house, "Any Montana men left?"

Someone answered, "Two."

"Tell 'em to hit the trail north now."

"You'd better join them, Britt," Martha said. "There's no place for you here. There never will be."

Britt said thinly, "Suits me. The farther away I am from you the better I'll like it." He wheeled and tramped off toward the bunk house and a horse.

Martha turned now to Webb. "Does that answer your question?"

"Did I ever ask one?"

"Yes. Not in words, but it was in your eyes. You wondered if I still loved Britt. Now do you know?"

"I reckon," Webb said slowly. "Was that the only question you saw that I didn't ask?"

"If you want an honest answer, no. I saw another," Martha said.

"Like to answer it?"

"Not before it's asked," Martha said.

Webb drew her to him and asked it.

DELL'S ACTION-PACKED WESTERNS

Selected Titles